I0818070

PRAISE FOR

Blood Wizard Chronicles Novella-Pononga

"Jay Erickson's writing is extraordinarily lucid and vivid. He entwines the story-line and the characters with uncanny detail and pragmatism, it makes you think you're truly watching Stormwind and his exploits! I found myself pondering what would happen next, and couldn't wait to get home from work to continue reading it! I highly recommend it!"

-George Kramer, author of the *Arcadis Fantasy Series*

Blood Wizard Chronicles Novella-Dark Consort

"The character of Stormwind is aptly named, as he floats in to people's lives and shakes them up in more ways than one! The author weaves a complex tale marrying classic heroism and mystery elements with modern ideas in a complex fantasy world. Stormwind's character acts as a catalyst, moving the action and keeping the reader guessing as to what might come next. Follow Stormwind's path and get a deep and exciting look into the culture, intrigue, and emotions of a unique race of Elves through this new novella from Jay Erickson."

-Anastasia Trekles, author of *Core*

"Jay Erickson spins a tale so engrossing it left me hungry for book 3 and thirsty to re-read book 1. An intriguing tale that maximizes characterization, instantly taking me into his world. Highest regards, you won't be disappointed."

-C.E. Rocco author and Editor-in-Chief, Old School Publishing

Blood Wizard Chronicles Novella-Stormwind

"*Stormwind* is an intense, character-driven melodrama that never ceases to be entertaining. It's heroes are immediately likeable and the action is vivid, but it has just enough substance to make the reader think. Plus, it has so many plot twists both M. Night Shyamalan and Christopher Nolan are jealous!"

-Nathan Marchand, author of *Pandora's Box* and co-creator of *Children of the Wells*

Blood Wizard Chronicles-Pariah

"*Pariah* is a fine example of intricate world-building with an interesting take on the standard fantasy tropes. A complex tale featuring adult themes and intriguing, relatable characters, it's a promising beginning to the *Blood Wizard Chronicles* series."

-C.S. Marks, author of *The Elfhunter Series*

"Readers who expect serialized cliffhangers in each chapter, popularized by authors like Dan Brown, may be disappointed. Instead Jay Erickson builds every moment to an intense conclusion, using graphical landscapes that are vivid and provide the backdrop to a powerful dialogue that drives the story. The emotional and psychological depth given to the characters shows that Jay Erickson is laying the groundwork for a growing future with each interaction."

-Brad Mitchell, PhD, MA, MS, Med. Associate Professor of Psychology and author of *Surviving Psychology*

Books by Jay Erickson

The Blood Wizard Chronicles-

Pariah
Recreant (Coming Soon!)

Blood Wizard Chronicles Novellas-

Stormwind
Dark Consort
Pononga

EXACTORS

TALES FROM THE CITADEL

Jay Erickson

and

J.P. Strohm

Edited by Kathleen LaSelle

HALSBREN
PUBLISHING, LLC

If you enjoyed this book, please take a moment to review it favorably.

EXACTORS: TALES FROM THE CITADEL

Edited by Kathleen LaSelle
Cover design and layout by Jay Erickson.
Additional art royalty free by FreeVector.Com

Published By: Halsbren Publishing LLC. *La Porte, IN. 46350*
ISBN: 978-1-942958-06-2
Made in the United States of America.

DEDICATION

To everyone who has given me so much enthusiasm and encouragement to continue to expand the ever growing world of Kuldarr.

To J.P. Strohm for showing so much interest in the lands of Kuldarr that he was willing to add his own stories to it. Thank you.

-Jay Erickson

~ ~ ~

I dedicate my first published work to all of my friends and family over the last thirty years. I appreciate all of your patience, blood, sweat, and tears (and yelling).

I never saw myself as a storyteller, just as a guy running a game. It is because of everyone of you that I am doing this for all too enjoy.

I thank Jay Erickson for his insight in this new realm I am running. Iniside I feel like the first time I gamed with my first group. I hope and pray you find these stories to your liking.

Finally I want to thank God and his Son, Jesus, for the opportunity to be myself, and allow me to share and express my creativity.

-J.P. Strohm

THE WEST
Auroral Sea
High Province
R. Eoi
R. T'Narg
Trinsen
Dupil
Gilhem
House Gönel
Wasteland
Order of the Sacred Fist
Agot
Impassable Range
Ethens
The Wilds
Strie-kÿr
Lugos Mountains
Malten
R. Provenan
Rhacotis
Halsbren
R. Ziibi
Gurgen
R. Faith
The Shemma
The Citadel
Featherset
Sowle Sea

THE EAST
Dire Plateau
Mystic City Ruins
Jaës
Oganis
Highfolk
Eratat Lake
Broken Teeth Mountains
R. Koba
R. Adnama
Buckner
Tilliatemma
Dakoria
Fermania
Czynsk
Shalis-Fey
Bremingham
Vesuvian Range
Sprigen
Gnomelaneum
Gnomesgate
Ire Ocean
Jay Erickson 2014
KULDARR

TABLE OF CONTENTS

INTRODUCTION

EXACTORS- they come from all walks of life. From vagrants to war heroes, from priests to sorcerers, from criminals to law enforcers. Some come from the streets seeking a chance at a better life. Others come from the noblest of houses seeking to establish their own legacy.

Exactors are the Jasian Enclave's dirty little secret. Contractors whose duty it is to complete the missions that the Church cannot openly admit to doing, or if they need an expendable asset. The range of such missions varies widely, as do the unique skills of the exactors.

Within these pages are the rare chronicled exploits of the exactors. They have been pieced together by recently found hidden documents, billing statements, ship manifests, trusted sources, and even hearsay. Each tale has been placed in chronological order by the date on which the events took place.

These dates, for your better understanding, have simply been tied to the widely known historical event, **STORMWIND**, which transpired with an Elf named Stormwind, and a monk of the Order of the Sacred Fist.

For the sake of clarity, it will be labeled with a generalized date, and about how long before, or after, the events that surrounded Stormwind took place

Not all actions performed by the exactors are nefarious, nor are they benevolent, but within these pages is a mixture of both. It shows the flexibility of the exactor, and why the Jasian Enclave needs them so...

-Aria Càidh
Chronicler of Jasian History

 JAY ERICKSON
J.P. STROHM

4848 E.o.E

SEVEN WINTERS PRIOR TO THE EVENTS OF STORMWIND

By:
Jay Erickson

PRELUDE

Bray couldn't move.

Fear, oppressive and heavy, like water-laden armor, weighed upon him. A set of menacing eyes looked at him, victorious. They wracked his body with terror as they came closer. Eyes that burned with an unholy green flame.

Bray wanted to raise his shield in defense. He wanted to pray to the Maker for his chosen deity's courage and blessings. He wanted to run. But he couldn't.

Paralyzed, and with an all-consuming dread, he watched, helpless, as it drifted towards him. A revolting, distorted head, suspended from insect-like wings. Around its ominous gaze was a crown of writhing tentacles all capped with wicked, barbed spines. Bray could see a pus-like fluid oozing from each of the dozen or so spurs.

The monster's mouth opened. He heard a loud pop and watched in disbelief as its jaws distended wide enough that it could enclose its maw completely around his own head. Jagged teeth slavered at the impending kill, and Aodhfin Bray knew without a doubt that he was doomed.

THE PROMOTION

72 hours earlier…

Sea spray misted his face, a squall of salty droplets that filled his nostrils and left a bitter taste on his tongue. He looked out across the deep blue waters spread out before him. Just at the edge of the horizon, he could make out the first signs of humanity since he, Aodhfin Bray, left the massive metropolis of the Citadel, heart of the Jasian Enclave.

Three weeks.

It had taken them three weeks. From initial notification to now, arriving just outside of the port town of Sentinel's Barrow had been twenty-one days. So much could happen in three weeks' time. What did they truly expect him to do?

Aodhfin's fingers brushed across the foreign locket at his neck. It was odd there. He wasn't used to wearing the bauble. He found it comforting though, and helpful in thinking, as he was doing now.

Twenty-one days.

Aodhfin Bray had been recently 'promoted'. It had not been one earned through meritorious service, but through blood; a field promotion.

A field promotion was not an odd thing for his chosen vocation of purist. He was a holy warrior for the church of the Maker, and bound to the doctrines of the Jasian Enclave. As such, violence was his way of life. He lived by conflict, and he knew he would one day die by it, as had happened to his commander.

What was odd, however, was that the attackers that he had fought had managed to infiltrate the Citadel itself. Usually all skirmishes with the Wilders, barbarians from the north, happened on the outer borders of the nation. The Citadel was nowhere near the conflict areas. It was located deep within Gurgen, far to the south against the deep waters of the Sowle Sea.

It was a bastion to the faithful. Its monolithic walls were supposed to keep all dangers out, and protect the pious within. For the Wilders to have managed to sneak within those massive hallowed walls... it was hard to fathom.

They had remained out of sight for weeks, eluding all patrols, civilizations, and even merchants. Well-organized and efficient, when they finally breached the Citadel walls, they had all the advantages. They might have been able to steal anything, or even kill one of the most powerful people in the world.

Each Wilder had known it was likely a suicide mission. Once within the Citadel it was a death sentence. Therefore, if they were going to track down and eliminate anyone within the religious conurbation it should be someone whose death would have been the most impactful and destructive to the religious imperium.

Instead, they sought to assassinate a woman. To Aodhfin this was vexing: Proffering to give up their own lives to kill someone of very little tactical merit.

While Jasia, martyr of the Maker, and his chosen daughter, was the cornerstone of their faith, no woman held any power within the Enclave. Not militarily, nor politically.

They had many sisters who led services and assisted in prayers. Women supplied themselves to trades of healing and alchemy, nursing and tradecraft. Yet none was allowed a position of any such significance that infiltrating one of the most heavily-fortified bastions in the world to kill her made any kind of sense. Yet they had done it anyway, and when questioned why, they had only uttered a single word.

Ambrosia.

Aodhfin did not know who or what Ambrosia was. No one in the Enclave did. The Wilders had taken this one and only chance to breach the Citadel's defenses, and they wasted it on a ghost.

The purists tracked and cornered the insurgents. Instead of learning more about Ambrosia, the Wilders fought and died, taking their knowledge of this Ambrosia to their graves.

It was no victory for Aodhfin. His commander and close friend, Ser Barodin Simonis, had been the first to fall at the assassins' skilled hands. Aodhfin took command of his unit, and with the loss of only two more purists he had eliminated the Wilders.

Three good men had died, and Aodhfin would likely never know why. Why these insurgents had risked everything, and killed Aodhfin Bray's brothers-at-arms for a single word.

Now, as the salty froth washed against his face once more, he thought of what he was going to say to Bishop Simonis when he saw him. His son was dead, slain within walls thought to be impenetrable. Yet more disturbing was that it had come at the most unfortunate time. Someone had contacted the Citadel for help within Sentinel's Barrow.

Of course, Aodhfin would come to their aide. It was all he could do. He dropped his hand from the locket and looked back to the stern of the ship. As part of his new role as purist commander, they had assigned him two exactors for the tasking.

Mercenaries.

Aodhfin felt his lip curl in disgust. He would have rather traveled with his unit, but Adjutant Daz had not thought it prudent. Though he was going to report the death of a devout purist to the family, the real reason he was here was to look into a murder, and possibly, if the missive he had received was correct, a haunting.

For that, he needed an exactor, a contractor that worked for the Jasian Enclave, but had no religious or political affiliation to it. The church exploited a loophole so that it may use sorcerers within its ranks. This way they still maintained abstinence from such magics itself, while not becoming victims from it. It was also a fortunate coincidence, because if the exactor was found doing something heretical, the church could 'wash their hands of it' and claim no connection.

The Enclave only permitted the healing and cleansing magic of **Creation** to be used while bearing the will of the religious nation-state. They were never allowed to bend creation for avarice, ever. However, an outside source, hired for a purpose, such as an exactor… well, that was a grey area.

Aodhfin did not care for the use of magic. He trusted in only three things: his faith in the Maker, the strength of his shield, and the quality of his skills to see him through. Relying on such an extraneous ability like magic seemed foolhardy. Why wield something that imparts a sacrifice on the user? Why weaken yourself on the field of battle and make yourself easy prey to an arrow or axe? Why control something that equally controls you?

He saw the sorcerer now, losing his last meal once more over the side of the vessel. Bray shook his head at the incompetent exactor. Perhaps the sorcerer should have learned a spell of stomach tranquility?

This 'magic man' was a High Elf from Trinsen, capital of the High Province, a nation so far north it was past even the Wilds. Aodhfin had never been there. Most of his life he had spent in Gurgen. Only when he became a purist had he started to see pieces of the world around him.

The Elf's name was Lotul Varthstone, and he claimed he was from a family of esteemed sorcerers. He touted that sorcery had been in his family for the last five millennia. Ever since the beginning of the Sixth Era; The Era of Enlightenment.

Aodhfin thought Lotul was an idiot. If this Varthstone was so good at using creation, then why was he so sick every day on the ship? Why couldn't he conjure sea legs?

Still, he knew that Lotul had other uses. Being a High Elf, or Goldhym, as they referred to themselves, afforded him sway with the other Elves that were within Sentinel's Barrow.

The port town was unique within Gurgen. It was the only town that supported an equal amount of humans, and Elves. Oddly enough, they had co-mingled harmoniously for many winters. At least until now…

The use of Lotul may sway some of the locals in his favor. Purists, though adored by many within Gurgen's borders, were also feared. They acted in the name of the Maker, and as such, operated as judge, jury, and executioner. This gave them a 'power' that left many uncomfortable. Luckily, purists were men of the Maker, and so they never abused such power, Aodhfin included.

Aodhfin also knew that Lotul had… features… that would enable him to associate well with the gentler side of the species. Many women considered his tall height, long and straight golden hair, pale skin, and smooth face attractive. The Elf also had a unique way of looking at the fairer gender with his hazel eyes. When he did, it seemed to make every woman he encountered blush and bat her lashes at him.

Aodhfin, himself, had no such need for frivolities. He knew his hooded blue eyes, pronounced brow, and strong set jaw were often found unappealing by the opposite sex. Had he not been raised in the confines of the Citadel it might have meant something, but as it stood, his facial traits mattered little to him. A purist lived a life for the Maker. He did not spend it sowing his oats with every willing participant he found. As dictated by the Jasian Enclave, a wife was selected for him by his family, or the Church.

Such a woman waited for him back at the Citadel now. One of the loveliest and most gifted creatures he ever had the luxury of meeting. She had soft dark hair that seemed impossible to control, and eyes the color of chocolate. She was fifteen winters old, and soon, on her sixteenth she would be his. The Maker smiled upon him for granting such a union. Soon they would be wed, and a proper, bountiful family would blossom in its wake.

Until that time, he would remain pure of heart and of body. He hadn't seen her in over a winter now. Not that it meant much. Often purists were gone for long periods. She had his heart, and that was all that mattered. After all, he had a job to do in the Maker's name.

He shook the thought of his lovely fiancée from his mind and called Lotul down from the stern. The pale Elf looked at him forlornly and shambled down the stairs, holding the side rail for dear life as the ship pitched up and down. Aodhfin thought the Elf looked green.

"Where is Sange?" he barked at the seasick Elf.

The sorcerer managed a weak shrug. "I'm not that bison's keeper. Find her yourself."

Aodhfin scowled at the pompous Elf, though he couldn't dispute his comparison of the large muscular woman with such a strong animal.

Sange was a massive and stout woman that stood taller than most men. She was young, like he, at only eighteen winters old. Her arms were thick with hard muscles, and she had a barrel of a chest, with breasts so small they might as well not exist. She wore simple leathers over her heavily muscled body, and favored a lumber axe as her weapon of choice. Were it not for the misleadingly soft round features of her face, with her large doe brown eyes, a button nose, and curvaceous lips, she could easily be mistaken for a man.

When Aodhfin had first been introduced to Sange, he thought that she was a Wilder. Yet she had grown up protected within the borders of Gurgen, in a small lumber-town on the edge of the Shemma Great Woods. He knew it explained the leathers and why she favored an axe, but it did little to answer her size.

Wilders were known to be upwards of seven feet tall, and she had to be almost that tall, perhaps a stone shorter. The purist had no doubt there was Wilder ancestry there, but if the Enclave accepted it, and she wasn't against fighting the northern hordes, then he too had no objection.

Besides, she favored skill and the strength of her arm over the powers of the mind. That was something she and Aodhfin agreed on.

Just as he was about to admonish the annoying sorcerer, Aodhfin heard a crash from below, followed by raucous laughter. Moments later the hatch flew open, and the large frame of Sange came climbing out, her trademark lumber axe tethered to her back. Blood trickled from her nose, but she wore a broad grin on her small shapely mouth.

Two more of the deck hands followed afterwards, each looking worse for the wear. Blood matted their hair, and scuffs marked their disheveled clothing. Already one of them had a swollen and darkening eye.

"Man, ye guys have some weird customs," the big woman's deceptively sweet voice intoned as she wrapped both of them in a bear hug once they were on deck.

"Ye were good fer da crew, Sange," black eye said."Ye eva wanna sail, ye come back!"

Sange nodded at them and then looked to Aodhfin. "I hear ye was lookin' fer me, Ser."

Aodhfin nodded. Though she was an exactor, she knew rank and station and afforded it to him. He appreciated that, considering that Varthstone knew no such respect. They were all here, and after three weeks of waiting, the time was upon him.

His eyes drifted once more to the green and brown mass that was now growing closer with every bob of the prow. The spires of the Enclave were in sight. Soon he would be ashore, and he would have to face Bishop Simonis and inform him of the fate of his son.

SIMONIS

Bishop Simonis was far from an imposing man. Standing almost a head shorter than Aodhfin Bray and stooped with the beginnings of a man entering his twilight winters, the pudgy holy man looked more like a settled sack of potatoes then the Enclave's resident leader.

Thin grey hair combed over a baldpate and jowls that resembled the neck of a chicken completed his look. His son had looked nothing like the man before him, and Aodhfin only hoped that he had gotten much of his looks from his mother.

Simonis' jowls wavered as he shook his head and spoke. "No," he said, "I did not request any purists. The Enclave is mistaken. Your time was wasted."

He dismissed Bray without a single glance from his droopy hazel eyes and sat back into his plush chair. "Now if you will excuse me, Purist Grey, I am a busy man."

"Bray," Aodhfin countered, not letting the man get to him. "I was told about a murder that needed solving, though. Adjutant Daz was rather insistent."

Simonis dismissed his comment with a wave of his hand. "Daz," he harrumphed. "That old coot thinks we can't do our job here well enough! We may not have purists stationed here at the Burrow, but we have an adjutant! Hells, we had two!"

"Two?"

Simonis nodded. "Man who was murdered was retired and living his last winters in peace. Good enough man, Vey Gallach was. It's a loss, truly."

"An adjutant was murdered and you feel that I'm not needed here?" Bray remarked, incredulous.

Simonis smiled condescendingly. "Contrary to what you believe young man, we are fully capable of solving crimes without purists, you know."

"He was an adjutant!"

"Retired," Simonis reiterated. "Besides, it was a cut-and-dried case. His wife, Esme, murdered him. She was found at the scene, weapon in hand. She had stabbed him multiple times. Blood coated her hands and the murder weapon. It was upon her body, and even sprayed the walls! Adjutant Murrough was the first responder. So, it was pretty clear. She killed her husband in a crime of passion."

"I see," Aodhfin said, tight-lipped. "So she's imprisoned then? I would much like to speak to her myself."

"That is not possible," Simonis retorted. "She killed an ex-adjutant. There's only one response for that, my boy, and you know that."

"What's he mean by that?" Sange asked from behind Bray.

"The rules for women are very clear," Simonis said sternly. "She murdered a man of the Maker in cold blood. She cast her own soul to the Defiler when she did so. The only pardon from such an act is to brighten her spirit once more in the hopes that the Maker will see something worth saving that we mere mortals cannot."

"What in the hells is that supposed to mean?" Varthstone asked, as tactless as ever.

"It means absolution through fire," Bray answered.

He looked at both Sange and Varthstone, who stared at him, confused.

"Esme is dead," he told them. "She was burned alive."

AUTHORITY

"What the hells is wrong with ye people!" Sange yelled at Simonis.

"Purist, control your exactors," Simonis replied calmly, not even addressing Sange.

Aodhfin raised his hand to silence Sange. Her eyes went wide with incredulousness. He ignored it, and spoke to the Bishop. "I would like to make inquiries, if I may?"

"Why?" Simonis asked, a shadow crossing over his features.

"As a purist assigned here by the Enclave, it is my responsibility to report that justice was dealt accurately. I just need to confer with your people and see the crime scene, and I will be out of your way."

Simonis nodded. "I can understand that," he answered, his turkey-neck wobbling. "Adjutant Murrough is at the garrison. I would recommend speaking with him first."

Bray nodded as well. "And who is the mortician responsible for handling the deceased?"

"Fem Fonzil."

"Fonzil is a High Elf surname?" Varthstone inquired.

The Bishop nodded. "It's not uncommon. You will find an equal mix of Elves and humans here, exactor."

"Did Ser Fonzil exhume both bodies?" Bray asked.

Simonis nodded.

"Where did the crime take place?"

Simonis looked out his window to the north. "Gallach Manor. Adjutant Murrough can direct you, or he can assign some of our local militia to assist you. Just don't go in there alone."

"Why?"

Simonis shifted in his lush chair uncomfortably. "Well, ever since Gallach died, the manor has been unwelcoming of people."

"Unwelcomin'?" Sange asked.

"It's haunted," Varthstone replied and then pointed a thumb at himself. "That's why I'm here."

Simonis scrutinized the Elf, "How did you…," his eyes snapped open wide. "Daria!"

He spat the name so quickly that Aodhfin almost missed it. "Who's Daria?"

Simonis waved his hand dismissively. "We're done here. If you want any more questions answered, I suggest you speak with Adjutant Murrough. I'm a very busy man."

"Who is Daria?" Bray repeated. He was beginning to grow concerned. Simonis was acting very strangely.

The Bishop growled at him. "Get out!" he yelled, "Or I'll have you removed! I am still in charge here, and an upstart purist and his team of thugs will not patronize me! I gave you authorization to speak to the others. You want answers, get it from them."

Aodhfin eyed the Bishop curiously as the man turned the color of a plum in his fury. Then he nodded.

"Let's go," he told the Exactors.

He bowed once to the Bishop. "Ser." Bray then extricated himself from the man's quarters. He would tell Simonis about his son's death later; right now he had a murder to solve.

~ ~ ~

"Animals," Sange muttered as they walked down the cobblestone path from the rectory of the Jasian Enclave and to the garrison where they hoped to find Adjutant Murrough.

"It is law," Bray answered. "She murdered a man of the cloth and darkened her soul. The only way to gain freedom from such a mar is to lighten it."

"They set er' on fire," Sange said through gritted teeth. "Burburic."

"I think what you meant to say was 'barbaric'," Lotul responded. "But, yes I agree."

"It is law," Bray said again simply.

"Would they burn a man alive if he had murdered a sister?" Varthstone asked.

Bray didn't answer.

As they approached the flat one-story structure of crème colored stone, Bray knew he was at the right spot. He had seen dozens of them, growing up in a family of purists. The outside of the garrison was plain, having no decorative crenellations or encrustations of any kind. Purists were men who lived without need for extravagance.

Square windows dotted the otherwise nondescript building, and a thick oak door was the only obvious entrance.

Before Aodhfin could reach for the door, it suddenly flew open. There in the doorway was an older man, perhaps in his late forties to early fifties. He was lean, with a sharp hooked nose, thin lips, and piercing blue eyes. Brown hair cascaded down around his shoulders and was covered by a feathered cap. On his chest, he wore the blue tabard embedded with a white circumpunct in the middle. The tabard was standard garb of the purist. Or in this case, an adjutant.

"Ser Murrough?" Bray asked.

The man raised an eyebrow. "And who are you, young man?"

Bray bowed. "Ser, my name is Aodhfin Bray, Purist of the Jasian Enclave, sent from Adjutant Daz to investigate the murder of Adjutant Gallach."

Bray could feel Murrough's scrutinizing gaze upon him. "The murder has been solved. Why would the Citadel send anyone?"

Bray shrugged, "That is what I am trying to find out as well, Ser."

Aodhfin studied the adjutant as the man looked over his shoulder to Sange and Varthstone behind him. "They issued you exactors, not additional purists?"

Aodhfin nodded, "Yes, ser."

"Well you will find few answers, I'm afraid. Esme was found guilty immediately and put to pyre." Murrough said as he moved around the young purist. Aodhfin fell into step beside him.

"So Bishop Simonis has informed me."

"Then there you have it," the adjutant said.

"I was wondering if I could ask you a few questions at least, so I can report back to the Citadel that justice was dispensed."

The adjutant didn't look at him as they walked. "Of course, purist."

"You were the first responder, correct?"

Murrough nodded at him. "Yes, I heard the screams of an argument and I went to investigate. My manor is across from theirs, you see."

"I see," Bray answered. "Did they argue often?"

"As much as any couple wedded to each other for so long. They wanted to kill each other daily."

Bray stopped walking.

Murrough turned to him smiling. "Sorry, poor humor. I jest," he shrugged. "They did fight some, yes. Nothing like I had heard that night though. Gallach was angry. He sounded loud and aggressive."

"Coulda she 'ave been defendin' herself?" Sange asked.

Murrough eyed her darkly. "Loud and aggressive does not mean violent," he snapped. "Vey Gallach was a good man. He did much for Sentinel's Barrow, and for the Enclave. He devoted winters of his life to countless crusades before becoming an adjutant and then settling down in this little port town. He was a hero."

"We did not mean to presume otherwise," Bray said as he scowled at Sange.

Murrough nodded. "It is a very sore subject for us," the man admitted. "We very much loved Esme, and Vey. Their deaths have impacted us all."

"Were you friends with Gallach?"

"I was there often."

"And you never saw any signs of malice between either of them?"

The Adjutant shook his head no. "Purists are above such things, remember?"

Bray nodded.

Murrough looked out over the horizon and the purist followed the man's gaze. In the distance, he saw a young woman, near his age, tending a garden. She had long black hair that shimmered in the sunlight, but her back was to them.

"Is there anything else, purist?" Murrough asked, impatient.

"One more question," Aodhfin said. "Who is Daria?"

Murrough's face scrunched in either disgust or anger, Aodhfin wasn't sure. He spat on the ground. "Her name is Daria Gallach.

"Gallach?" Bray asked.

"By birth she's Vey and Esme's daughter."

WHEEL

"What do you mean, by birth?" Bray asked.

Murrough, now impatient to move on, looked Bray in the eyes. "She has disavowed the Maker, and no longer considers herself one of his children. She's a pagan and a heretic now."

Aodhfin was shocked. He had never heard of such a thing, at least not from a child of an adjutant. Once in a family as committed to the Maker as purists and adjutants were, always committed.

"Who does she worship now?" Sange asked behind him, unmoved by the adjutant's words.

"Non-committal as far as I know, though I couldn't really care less," he said dismissively. "Now really purist, I have things to do."

Bray nodded. "I understand," he answered with a bow of his head. "Thank you for your time, Ser."

Murrough moved around him quickly, and Bray asked one last question. "Where is Daria now?"

Without looking back, he answered, "No one in this town really cares." Then he was gone, heading towards the young woman tending her garden.

~ ~ ~

"I'm not really getting a very cozy vibe here," Varthstone commented with a dour expression on the evening of their second day.

They sat around a small table in an inn called the Penitent Wheel. It was a well-made structure, complete with a full tavern, twin fireplaces, and huge, lavishly decorated rooms full of fineries that Bray would never have a need for. It was the type of lodging reserved for wealthy merchants, or visiting dignitaries. It wasn't Bray's first choice, but he didn't want to stay in an obvious location and project his comings and goings so openly to Adjutant Murrough.

Bray chose not to answer Varthstone's statement, but instead stared at his pint of amber ale in front of him. There was nothing to say. He felt that things seemed off as well. They had questioned various townsfolk for two days on the events that led up to the murder of Gallach, and then Esme's execution. To all of them it seemed matter-of-fact. Esme sinned heavily and she paid the price. The fact that she was set ablaze before Gallach's body even had a chance to cool didn't seem to concern them one bit.

Furthermore, no one wanted to help in locating Daria. Like Adjutant Murrough had proclaimed, no one cared. When she turned her back on the Maker, she turned her back on them.

Her actions angered Aodhfin as well. He believed strongly in his god, he believed in the good of the Enclave. For her to turn away from that, after her father had given so much…

"Why are we 'ere?"

Bray looked up, his anger at Daria momentarily interrupted.

"Why are we 'ere?" Sange quipped again, taking a particularly long draw from her pint. She wiped the froth off her lips with the back of a gloved hand. "The Bishop dinna contact us like the Enclave said, and the case has been solved, haddin' it? I mean, horrific-ally, brutitally, savagely solved, but solved," she added, her discontent for the way the wife had been treated seeping through each word.

"Aye," the sorcerer agreed. "Good point. Though, it's 'horrifically', and 'brutally'. You'll learn how to speak like the big boys one day."

Varthstone ignored her withering glare, facing Bray. "What are we still doing here, Purist? I mean ships still in port an' all, we can hop a ride back to the Citadel, report what you found, and none's the wiser."

Sange nodded her agreement, though her look didn't change.

"Just like that?" Bray asked. "A man was murdered, a daughter is missing, and the wife, executed for the crime. All of this doesn't strike you as a little odd?"

"Sure it does," the Elf agreed. "But we're not here for that, we're here for a murder. That's solved. Wife did it." The way he said 'Wife did it' made Bray pause. It didn't sound like he meant it.

"You think she was innocent?" Aodhfin asked.

Varthstone gave a little shrug. "It's not my place to question my employers, but since you're asking, no I don't think she did it. It's like you said, it's a little odd, and a bit too convenient if you ask me."

"I dunna like how everyone jus' accepts it," Sange added. "I mean, Gallach had been here fer a long time right? Did they all hate him or sumtin'?"

"He was an adjutant, and before that, a purist," Bray stated.

"So he was a dick," Sange said.

Bray glowered at her, but it quickly faded when he saw the large smile on her face.

"Yer so serious all the time!" she said jovially, before adding, "I jus' think it's a mite bit odd is all, how they're jus' going about it like nuthin' happened."

"It's almost been a month," Bray interjected.

"Yeah, imagine if someone close to ye died less than a month ago, how would ye feel?" she asked.

Bray winced. He realized how he did feel and Sange was right: they *were* too callous. Why?

"There's also still the matter of the haunting," Lotul's almost songlike voice explained. "We were sent here to tend to that, too."

Bray didn't answer. He stared at the white head bobbing gently atop the crisp golden liquor. Barodin's death hurt him, and they had only been friends for a few winters. Simonis and Murrough had to have known Gallach for decades. Worse, Simonis didn't want them here, and Murrough seemed to not care less. It may be their way of dealing with the grief, but Bray didn't think so. That meant there was someone out there who did care. Someone who left that had the authority to request the dispatch of a purist to properly solve the case.

The exactors continued.

"Who cares 'bout tha place? Suren' the Enclave here doesn't. An' if the daughter's been estranged then she has no rights to it," Sange said matter-of-factly."Right?"

Varthstone shrugged. "Not my area of expertise. I don't know what would be needed to claim rights."

Then Bray understood. He understood what was happening and why someone had reached out to the Citadel. "They're cutting her out."

Both exactors looked at him. "They don't want a heretic to assume the property. Property owned by a devout man of the cloth. It's a slap in their collective faces." A dawning of comprehension engulfed him. "A will. They need a will."

"Who does?" Sange asked.

"Anyone. Everyone," Bray replied, his energy levels rising. "Gallach's last will and testament will direct who all the assets belong to after he died. Likely it was his wife, but if he put a secondary recipient or even a tertiary…"

"And if there is no will?" Varthstone inquired.

"Then the property and all its fortunes turn over to the Enclave."

Varthstone nodded, "Which in this case is Simonis."

"Even though Daria is still a living heir?" Sange asked, disbelievingly.

Bray nodded, "It is irrelevant. All purists, adjutants too, are required to have a will once they wed. If they don't then all their worldly possessions are subject to the Enclave."

"What kind of timeline are we looking at for that?" Varthstone asked. "Months? Winters?"

"Twenty-five days," Bray replied.

Sange spit her drink out in surprise. "What?"

Aodhfin nodded. It made sense, why they didn't want him here, why they didn't want the exactors around. Everything was falling in place right where they needed it. Everything was just so convenient.

A husband killed by his wife. A conviction and execution immediately follows. A daughter branded a heretic and separated from the church. Brand the home haunted so no one would search it for the will, and you have no clear recipient to the estate. They only needed to hold it like that for twenty-five days, and the Citadel would legally honor all dividends sent to Simonis and the clergy.

Bray didn't want to believe it. He didn't want to think that this was what Simonis may be plotting. A man of the church, a man devoted to the Maker. Nevertheless, something was clearly afoot. There was a reason they were not wanted here. He hoped to the Maker that he was wrong, and it was all a big mistake. Yet he couldn't deny the coincidence, or the fact that no one really seemed that upset over the loss of Gallach and his wife. Bray was short on leads and this seemed like as good as any.

"We have less than forty-eight hours," Bray said.

"Fer what?" Sange asked.

Bray looked at her and felt a certainty in what he need do. “To find the will and find out who really stood to gain by the deaths of Vey Gallach and his wife.”

MANOR

"Where do we even begin ta look?" Sange asked, shaking her head.

"Logic says Daria," Bray answered. "She stands to gain the most if the will surfaces."

"No one'll tell us where ta find Daria, and I canna track a ghost in a town full of people," Sange replied.

"Then let's track the ghosts themselves," Varthstone said.

Bray looked at the High Elf. Lotul shrugged, "It's why I'm here, right? I mean aside from my good looks."

Sange rolled her eyes.

"No, he's right," Bray said, looking at the two of them, a plan percolating in his head. "Adjutant Daz picked a sorcerer to deal with a possible haunted manor. I'm no expert on haunting and personally I don't believe in them, but if they do exist then…."

"A miffed spirit migh' tell us where the will is?" Sange asked, not believing her own words.

Varthstone chuckled. "They are more likely to kill you through possession of your muscles, forcing every part of your body into a series of crippling seizures, until it grips your lungs, ruptures blood vessels, and fills them, causing you to drown in your own blood. If you're lucky though, they'll clot your blood instead, and it rushes to your brain. Pop! No more Sange. Or, in the state of your convulsions, you might break your own neck. That would be best I think," he remarked nonchalantly.

Sange fixed Varthstone with a murderous stare.

"I was going to say we should be wary," Bray told them both, ending any debate before Sange pummeled the skinny Elf. "Personally I think it's a trick to keep everyone out of the manor. Once it transfers over to Simonis, I'm sure the ghosts will suddenly just vanish."

"And iffin' it's not?" Sange asked.

"Then I do what I'm paid for," Varthstone said with a smile.

~ ~ ~

An hour later, the trio stood before the large portcullis to Gallach Manor. It was almost pitch black out. A heavy cloud cover drowned out the few stars that dotted the sky, and it happened to be the first night of a new moon.

A blackened iron fence stood eight feet high and ran completely around the perimeter of the property. Before them, the gate hung open only a few inches. It swayed ominously on creaky hinges even though there was no wind. There was a large G gilded onto both sides of the gate in gold. It seemed dull and muted in the dim night.

Bray stared at the gilding, the corners of his eyes etched with concern.

"Second thoughts?" Sange asked as she stared morosely into the void-like courtyard beyond.

He shook his head no. "I'm just wondering how an adjutant, who is supposed to turn away from all worldly possessions, could live in a large manor, with a golden engraved gate?"

"Well, he was retired," Varthstone reminded Bray. "Could that make a difference?"

"I suppose," he agreed.

"Perhaps it's plain in der. Like a monastery." Sange queried. "Or maybe this was one of the only structures they could give 'im at the time."

Bray shot her a patronizing look. She merely shrugged in mock innocence. Slowly he opened the gate and stepped into the courtyard beyond.

Due to the gloominess outside, the manor loomed in front of them like an opaque silhouette. In front of the dusky structure, Aodhfin heard the sounds of trickling water but couldn't quite make out the source.

Their feet crunched against loose pebbles on the cobbled path. Aodhfin noted that everything else was silent. No calls from insects, or hoots from owls, or cries from an errant fox. There was nothing, only the sounds from his feet, the water in front of him, and the heavy breathing behind.

"Well this is cheery," Varthstone said sardonically from behind. "Perhaps we should reconvene when we can see, like the daytime?"

Aodhfin ignored him as they moved forward. They had less than two days to solve a murder or find the will. The obvious choice is that Simonis must have it stowed away trying to hide it until the twenty-five days passed, but Aodhfin didn't think so. If they had it, they wouldn't be going through the ruse that Gallach Manor was haunted. If Daria had it, she would have come forward by now, unless she was dead, and if it was in someone else's possession they were keeping very quiet about it. That left the manor. If any clues were going to point them in the right direction, it would start here.

Abruptly the fountain came into view. It was flat and simple in design. A single round wall rose from the ground, constructed of white marble, and had no ornamentation of any kind. In the center of the pool of water was a raised platform of about four feet. From the top water trickled over, creating curtains of raining crystal clear liquid in a circular pattern down the pedestal and into the pool below.

Ivy had begun to grow over the walls of the fountain, and reached into the edges of the water, like extended fingers stretching for nourishment.

Bray walked up and looked into the pool of water. It was still clear, even in the black of night. Nothing had begun to obscure the waters yet. Again, something didn't sit right. Twenty-three days since Gallach died, the house was vacant, and yet someone was still cleaning algae from a fountain?

He continued through the courtyard until the obscure home came into view. Bray had not ventured so far north in Sentinel's Barrow during the day so he hadn't really gotten to see the estates. Seeing it now though, much like the gate, filled him with anger.

It was a mansion. Distinctive features of the white plaster façade included a massive entablature, and cornices lined with dentils. A row of square, giant order columns on granite bases supported the front. Twelve in all, these columns formed a double gallery. The front staircase had twin sets of stairs on both sides leading upwards toward the open gallery.

No adjutant should live so lavishly.

They carefully climbed the stairs to the gallery above. Bray could see several tall, floor-to-ceiling windows across the gallery's level. They inspected every one, finding them all locked, and heavy crème draperies pulled tightly shut. With no light source evident, the inside of the manor seemed as murky inside as the opaque night that surrounded them.

The trio advanced to the wide cherry wood door. A large custom black iron knocker was installed on the door, and Bray was relieved to see that it, at least, represented the Jasian Enclave.

The knocker was the symbol of Jasia herself. A statuette carved as a beautiful human woman, but bearing features similar to every devoted race. Her height and physical stature were just neutral enough that she could resemble a taller lithe Dwarf, or a slightly buxom Elven woman. To accent this she wore only a simple full-length garment, cinched at the waist. Jasia's hands were clasped together in reverence, for her father above.

She was the mortal daughter of the Maker, the one he had chosen to show the world that Creation is the will of one god, the Maker, not the many. In the end, she was a martyr, sacrificing herself for her beliefs. That sacrifice solidified the true birth of her religion, ultimately turning her fledgling belief into one of the most influential empires on all of Kuldarr.

Seeing that symbol filled him with a glimmer of hope that perhaps not all had been lost with Gallach. Perhaps the adjutant held dear to his principles more than the ostentatious house dictated. Bray wouldn't know of course until he entered the house. He reached out, grabbed the door handle, and pulled.

It didn't budge.

He tried to push on the door, and received the same result.

"Perhaps we should knock?" Varthstone quipped. "How do you use this thing anyway?" The sorcerer went up to the knocker and grabbed the small iron bosoms of the device.

Eyes wide, Bray slapped Varthstone's hands away. Sange snickered behind him. "How dare you desecrate Jasia in such a manner!" the purist seethed.

"You need to calm down, Commander," the Elf retorted, his lips dripping with a mocking woe. "I merely was trying to find that special spot that would open her up."

Sange's snicker turned into a full blurt of laughter. Bray looked incredulously at the two of them. "We are here to try and solve a murder, in the middle of the night, on the doorstep to a manor that might be haunted, and you make jokes? About my faith nonetheless! Are you really as stupid as you look, or is this all just an act to try and see how far you can push me?"

The sorcerer's jeering face fell flat at his eyes condescendingly glared at the purist. "It would not be wise to call a master of **Creation** stupid, priest."

Bray's hand slid to the handle of the war-hammer at his side. Aodhfin's voice was just as icy. "And I would be wary, were I you, of how you choose to act about my religion."

They stared at each other for several moments. Bray could feel the tension rising between the two of them, like a malevolent heat on a midsummer's day. The purist's fingers wrapped around the rough leather banding of the war-hammer's handle. A single phrase, a strange word uttered, and Bray would strike before the sorcerer could finish. They were too close to one another. The Elf would never be able to finish his spell.

Bray could see the same realization being calculated in Varthstone's eyes. The sorcerer knew he couldn't win. Not here.

Instead, he smiled. "Well, I'm glad we've gotten that out of the way then." Slowly he raised his hand to the door. "After you then, purist. Let's see if your god can open the way."

Aodhfin just released his grip from the hammer when, without warning, Sange's large muscular leg lanced forth. Her foot slammed into the door with bone-jarring force, causing whatever was barring the way to splinter and shatter. The door swung inward violently.

"Ye men take too long," she huffed as she stepped inside.

Bray shook his head in frustration. He hated exactors. They had no tact, and no control. Hells, they were damn near untrainable. He wished his unit were here with him, instead of this pathetic lot. They knew how to respond to the situation. His old leader could have handled Varthstone and Sange, he told himself bitterly. Angry beyond words, with more than just the exactors, he followed the mountain of a woman inside.

~ ~ ~

With no light outside and nothing forthcoming from the vacant building, the foyer was so incredibly black that if possible, Bray actually thought it looked blue.

"And we're back to being blind again," Varthstone remarked dryly.

As if his words conjured some mystical spell, suddenly the door slammed shut behind them, sealing them within the absolute darkness.

"What did ye do?" Sange hissed.

"Nothing!" Varthstone spat, a tinge of fear in his voice. "I did nothing!"

Bray wrapped his fingers around his war-hammer and carefully lifted it off the hook at his belt. He felt the weight of it in his hands. He felt more secure when he held his weapon. More alert. He calmly asked, "Did anyone glimpse anything at all before the door closed?"

"No," the hulking warrior woman replied.

"You're joking, right?" The sorcerer replied, "It was too dark *before* the door shut!"

Bray could tell from the timbre of his voice and his erratic breathing that the Elf was close to losing it. Bray had experience in morale failure. He had felt it the first time he was in combat. He had seen it with new recruits. A panicked soldier could break down a whole formation. It was the weakest link of every chain, and often the first thing to fail. When one went, a cascade of fear and failure followed. He didn't need Sange to lose her composure as well. Bray willed himself to remain passive and neutral as he told the Elf to calm down, that everything would be alright. He didn't allow a tremor to sneak into his voice; he didn't let his own turmoil affect his words. Barodin had always shown him strength, when Bray had flagged. The purist had to do the same now.

"Okay," he heard the sorcerer say, his voice already evening out.

He knew the tranquility of his voice had given the Elf a measure of courage. Now he needed to hold on to it. "Can you find the door?"

"Yes," Varthstone replied.

"Does it open?"

Bray heard it rattle and shake violently. He knew the answer before the Elf even replied, no. "Then we find another way. There are tall windows all around us, we are not trapped in here, we can leave at any time," he said simply. "For now let's set out to complete what we planned on doing."

"We've no light," Varthstone said.

"On it," Sange replied deftly.

Bray heard a clamoring behind him, followed by a loud rip of fabric. Moments later, there was a crash with a litany of curses.

"Sange?"

Without warning fire erupted to life only a few feet in front of him. "Sorry!" Sange apologized. "I dinna know we 'ere so close!"

She moved the open flame from his face and he could see immediately what she had done. Sange had found her way to one of the windows Aodhfin had mentioned, and ripped down the drapes and dowel that had held them in place. She tore long runners from the drapes and wrapped them around the dowel, and had somehow found a way to ignite the material.

"I keep a snifter of oil on me at all times," Sange said, reading the question in his eyes. "And flint."

"Clever girl," Bray returned. Now armed with light, they had a better look at their surroundings.

The foyer was large and circular shaped. The inside walls were lined with rounded ornate columns. Between each column on the south end were the tall windows. As Bray's eyes continued around the room he watched it transition from windows to doors, and finally at the northernmost point were another set of twin stairs. Beneath those stairs was a fireplace and mantle.

The ceiling sat an easy fifteen feet above them, affording him the ability to see a portico on the next floor that led to rooms beyond. Stone-encrusted balustrades protected the portico above.

Bray focused on the fireplace. It was massive, and the mantle and trim around it appeared to be made of marble. Like the balusters above, it held the same stone encrustations.

Bray's and Sange's attention became riveted to what was above the mantle. There on the wall was a full-scale portrait of Esme. What surprised him though, was not the fact that there was a portrait, but how amazingly beautiful the woman was.

A low whistle sounded behind him, conveying his more impure thoughts. Thoughts he quickly pushed from his mind.

"Now that's a looker," Varthstone said.

Bray even saw Sange nodding in agreement.

"And they put her to torch?" the Elf continued. "Such a waste."

Strangely enough, Aodhfin agreed with the sorcerer. Her beauty was a rare kind. Exotic, with black hair that was long and full. It flowed luxuriously down to the small of her back.

Vibrant emerald green orbs that were almond shaped glittered at them. High cheekbones, a thin nose, and full lips rounded out all the high points of her looks, but it was her jawline that he found, strangely, the most alluring. She had a strong jaw, almost like a man's. It was full with a square chin. Normally, Bray would have found such a thing almost too masculine, marring natural feminine beauty. On her though, it seemed… perfect. It gave her a presence that was hard to ignore. Just the sight of her was mesmerizing, and it was merely a painting.

Underneath her were the name Esme Gallach, and a date. The painting was only two winters old.

"How old was Gallach?" Sange asked, looking with concern at the picture.

Bray shrugged. He didn't know.

"This girl looks like she's in er' mid-twenties," Sange remarked. "I was a guessin' Daria was grown, by the way people spoke."

"As did I," Bray agreed. "Even if she married when she was sixteen, as is Enclave tradition, the daughter couldn't be more than what… ten, maybe eleven?"

"We need ta find that will," Sange said a little desperately. "No child deserves ta be made poor afta losin' their parents."

Again, Bray found himself in agreement with the exactor. It was wrong what they were doing to this child, regardless of belief, but was it true?

Bray still couldn't think that the Bishop was capable of such a dark act, yet with nothing else to go on he found he couldn't refute it, either. Simonis was involved with the murder in some capacity. It was up to Bray to find out just how involved.

HAUNT

They moved through the house for the better part of the next hour. Sange created two more torches for Bray and Varthstone out of the rest of the drapes and the legs off a chair from the dining room. As Bray held the sturdy polished oak in his left hand, he didn't even want to think how expensive the chair might have been.

They had tried to light the sconces on the walls, as well as the fireplace itself, but there was no good wood remaining, nor was there enough oil. So they traveled through the dark house as if it was some sort of dungeon and they intrepid adventurers.

Now Bray didn't think highly of exactors-- he thought they were all jackboots and thugs--and up until now, that impression had held. Yet he was surprised to see the two with him now move with purpose. As they inspected room after room on the first floor, they passed up countless valuables, from fine china, to jewelry, to expensive baubles that seemed to have no purpose, all likely to fetch a decent sum of money to the perceptive entrepreneur. Yet even the sharp-tongued sorcerer seemed determined to do his job. As much as he didn't like to admit it to himself, their dedication impressed him.

After checking every room on the first floor and the cellar, they found nothing that could even give a remote hinting towards a will or marital problems. There were portraits of the two of them, the adjutant and his wife, throughout the manor, and they looked happy. Bray supposed such things could be deceiving, with a dark reality bubbling underneath the surface of the beautifully painted works of art.

Outside of the door slamming and locking them in, they had not encountered any poltergeists of any kind. Bray had almost convinced himself that it must have been the wind. Almost. It was on the second floor that things began to change.

Bray led the formation as they moved up the gently winding stairs to the second floor. Halfway up he caught a movement by the balusters out of the corner of his eye. He wheeled the torch in the direction of the movement, red-orange light sputtering.

Sange drew her axe at his sudden turn. "What?" she whispered.

Bray shook his head. There was nothing there. Nothing at all.

"It's... nothing," he finally relented. "Let's go."

The purist stepped onto the portico, gingerly, as a feeling of worry began to grow in his gut. Something was different on this floor. He looked to his exactors. If they felt it too, they did not show it.

Lavish furniture dotted the backs of the walls, and Bray was forced to make a choice between the door on the left, and on the right. On the other floors, that hadn't mattered to him, they just split up to cover more ground. Now the twisting he felt in his innards only brought apprehension.

He decided left.

As the three of them walked through the doorway, all hell broke loose.

~ ~ ~

A blood-curdling scream sliced through the air and cut into the trio like daggers in their flesh. It was earsplitting and guttural. Bray immediately raised his hammer, ready for whatever was about to attack.

Varthstone spun around frantically. "Behind us... the stairs!" he yelled, raising a hand in defense.

"Over there!" Sange screamed, pointing at the opposite door on the portico just as it slammed shut.

Bray too saw something in front of him, a shimmering form in his flickering amber glow. It looked like a woman in a soft chemise. It hugged her sultry form as she moved forward towards him. Bray closed his eyes. *I do not believe in ghosts*, he told himself. *I do not believe in ghosts.* He opened his eyes.

She was still there.

She looked at him sorrowfully, her emerald green eyes pouring themselves over him like a pitcher of ice-cold water.

He felt himself shaking. "No," he growled. Bray stepped forward.

Suddenly the wraith screamed a banshee's wail once more. Her body erupted into flames and she ran down the hallway.

Bray turned to see if it had been the work of the sorcerer, but he saw immediately that it was not the case. Lotul was busy fighting his own phantoms. Flickering shards of ice flew out towards the balustrades from his extended fingertips. Lotul's torch lay on its side on the ground. The flame guttered. What the Elf was fighting, Bray couldn't see.

Sange was across the portico slamming her axe into the heavy door over and over again, like a lumberjack chopping down a tree. She seemed enraged, screaming so hard her vocal cords were tearing. Wood splintered with every massive impact from her muscle-laden arms. She would be through the door in no time, the purist reasoned.

Then Bray felt cold. Something like ice water rushed down his spine. He froze in place, and yet something turned him, controlled him.

He faced back down the hallway and she was there again, the spirit. Bray recognized her. She was the same lovely creature that he saw in the portrait downstairs. Esme.

She beckoned him forward with a thin ivory finger. Woodenly, his muscles reacted, convulsing in pain as he fought it. First he made one step, then another.

Esme took a step backwards, her eyes like viridian fire never leaving his face. They went down the hallway together, and Bray had no choice but to leave his companions behind, fighting their own battles.

He turned down another hall, and then turned again. Before he knew it, he was facing towards the courtyard once more. A towering picture window showed him the night beyond.

Esme reached out and touched the window. Frost ran across the pane of glass from her fingertip. It spread throughout the window like a spider's web. A weave of glittering crystals danced along its surface, reflecting like a thousand diamonds against the amber light of his torch.

Then the window was full, the bitter frost encased the whole sheet of glass like a veil. Bray heard the high-pitched whine of the thin windowpane followed by a snap.

Where Esme touched the pane was a small crack. There was a sheering sound and within a fraction of a second Bray watched, helpless, as the long lines arced and crisscrossed against the frost-laden panel.

It exploded. Shards of sharpened icy glass flew outward like glimmering daggers into the darkness of night. Immediately, warm, salty air slapped his face. In the distance, he could hear the thunderous roll of waves as they crashed ashore.

Bray felt his legs moving once more. One step. Another. He struggled against the feeling, his legs cramping and trembling. He wanted to scream in pain, but he couldn't fight it. She was too strong. He stepped up against the frame. He dropped his hammer to the ground and reached out to steady himself. His bare hand leaned against the sharp, cold glass. It bit into his flesh. Bray ignored the burn of the piercing shard that coursed through his hand. His sole concern was on the ground that loomed up at him from twenty feet below.

Hard cobblestones glared up at him expectantly. Aodhfin knew he had to win this fight, but she was so strong. Then his eyes fell to the fountain beneath him. He could now see that the flat simple design from below was actually a circumpunct, the symbol of the Jasian Enclave.

The purist prayed to the Maker for strength. He fought against the spirit with all he had. His muscles rippled in strain underneath his armor. His body quaked as he tried to deny her his body. His right foot lifted, and he felt himself lean forward. His whole body pitched forward, and the ground below was all he saw as the wind blew against his face. His torch toppled forward, cartwheeling out below him until it struck the ground in a flash of sparks. And then he was falling out after it.

THE SCENE

Thick arms like tree trunks wrapped around him just as his feet broke the plane of the windowsill. "Bray!" the voice bellowed in alarm. "Bray!"

His feet slammed back down against the frame, but his doeskin boots shuffled and slid forward. Aodhfin's mind was a haze. He couldn't muster any thoughts except that he was falling. Esme threw him from the window! He was falling!

"Pull him back," another voice said through the murk. There was a songlike eloquence to it. "Stupid, idiot purist."

Aodhfin watched in alarm as the ground pulled away from him. Slowly he was drug backwards until he saw a cherry wood frame shrouded with fragments of broken glass. One of them was covered in blood.

There was a loud groan as the big arms wrapped around his chest tighter and fiercely yanked him up and over. Then he was falling again, this time backwards as he toppled onto the person who had stopped him from jumping.

His head slammed against the wall as they fell, jarring him and causing the room to spin. A ringing sound echoed in his ears.

Aodhfin fell against something soft. It was supple and velvety against the side of his face.

"Do ye mind?" a distinctly feminine voice asked.

Aodhfin blinked several times trying to shake away the disorientation. He raised his head slowly, and was alarmed to see Sange's doe brown eyes looking down her nose at him only a few inches away.

It was then that Aodhfin realized where he landed. Sange's bosom. Or what she had of one anyhow. He pulled up quickly, embarrassed. "Sorry," he muttered.

Sange smiled.

The sorcerer behind them snickered. "You can get a room together later," he remarked snidely. "In the meantime, gather your wits purist. We're here."

Bray shook the cobwebs from his head. "Here?" he questioned. "But Esme! Watch for her spirit!"

He was surprised to see Lotul shaking his head. "I'll explain later, priest. Right now we have a crime scene to case." The sorcerer pointed to the room next to them.

Aodhfin followed the Elf's finger through the doorway, and he saw it clearly. The master bedroom. The place where Esme had killed Gallach.

The purist stood and extended his hand to help the large woman up. They both saw it running red with blood. "Bray!" Sange said in alarm.

Aodhfin pulled his hand back as the bitter sting suddenly began to throb throughout is hand. "It's nothing," he remarked. Aodhfin looked into a satchel on his belt and quickly removed gauze to wrap it. He kept it for such a purpose. When done, he hefted up his hammer and put it back on the hook at his waist.

He followed Varthstone into the room.

"Don't touch anything," he reminded them, though it seemed that the sorcerer needed no such prodding. It was apparent that he knew his way around a crime scene.

The room was large, at least half the size of the foyer. The floors were all a cherry wood, and the walls a crème stucco plaster. It was very different from the other rooms they had encountered. Cozy.

Against the east wall were two large windows. Not the full-size windows he had seen in the foyer, but smaller, only running from two feet off the ground to about eight feet high. White sheer curtains hung wistfully between crimson silk drapes. Out those windows, he could see the winking lights of lanterns half a mile away. Adjutant Murrough's estate.

Bray directed his gaze to the perimeter of the room. Chaise lounges dotted the four corners, each with ornate engraved end tables between them. A 'G' was hand embroidered into each one. Every chair seemed to be made of suede, and colored the same crème color as the walls.

A large fireplace adorned the southern wall.

In the center of the room was the bed. A massive four-poster that held a thick feather mattress and a dozen goose down pillows, all of them covered in silk sheeting the same crimson as the drapes. There were no dressers, chests, or armoires for clothing, nor were there closets of any kind. There was an attached room directly next to them, but Bray could see it led to a bathing area.

This wasn't a standard bedroom for a retired adjutant looking to slumber within. This room was a shrine.

Aodhfin could only stare. This was not how an adjutant was supposed to live his life in service of the Maker.

The purist's eyes drifted to where the altercation had taken place, directly next to the bed. Dried blood, now brown and flaky, had sprayed violently against the walls. There was a similar jet of crusted blood against the left foot poster of the bed. This had apparently run rich, as the sheets in that corner were soaked liberally. The overturned chair was adorned with bloodied handprints. On the floor an oblong, brown stain was now soaked into the pores of the wood. At the center of that stain sat a long-bladed dagger, jewel-encrusted, and covered up to the hilt in the dried morass.

Small feminine fingerprints could be seen across the room, on the dagger, the chaise, the bed, and even an end table. All, presumably, from the victim's blood.

Sange said what they all were thinking."Tis a lot of blood."

"Too much," Varthstone replied as he walked around the throne-like bed.

Without touching anything, he pointed to the walls. "You see the spray pattern here," he explained. "She hit a major artery. Otherwise, there should be no reason for such a projection. Look how high and far it reaches, look at the arc pattern," he pointed out. "She knew exactly what she was doing, in which case this is now premeditated. A crime of passion is sudden. A burst of unexpected violence. Anger and frustration are equal tools just as any dagger may be. There are repeated stabbings. This causes the blood to gush, or pour, not spray. Normally, the aggressor would get doused more liberally, and anything within direct proximity, say the bed. To me this room appears staged."

Aodhfin looked at the Varthstone in surprise. "Staged?"

The Elf nodded. "In the High Province, we call this an orgy of evidence. Look at the clues laid out for us to see, still untouched, due to the 'convenience' of the haunting."

"But it is haunted."

Again, Varthstone shook his head. "I'll explain later. In the meantime we focus on this murder."

Bray nodded. The exactor was right. He needed to focus on what was in front of him.

"Why is dis' 'ere an orgy?" Sange asked.

Varthstone smiled in his condescending way. "I'm glad someone is paying attention." He pointed to the dagger on the floor. "So our murderer thrusts this weapon into her husband, for argument's sake severs an artery, and then what? In a true crime of passion, she would keep stabbing, randomizing the pattern of arterial spray. Or freak out and either try to stem the bleeding, or flee. We know she didn't run, so why didn't she use the bedding to soak up the blood? Look at the patterns of the blood, precision strikes. Look where her 'handprints' are all located. What was she doing? Crawling?"

He pointed to the floor where the stain was greatest. "Let's just say it was a kill shot. She goes numb at what she did, so she just drops the dagger next to the body? Then she remains standing until she is apprehended, barefoot, at that."

"How?" Sange began, but Bray quickly answered. "Look at the stains on the floor, just out of the puddle," he said. "There are slight impressions, seven per step. Five for toes, one for the pad, the other for the heel. She has arched feet. A boot or slipper would be a single impression."

"Precisely," Varthstone replied. "Yet look at the rest of the floor. No other tracks, no foot prints at all, yet we have a bevy of handprints everywhere. Handprints being the easiest to compare to the alleged killer. Yet how could those handprints, which are more than likely Esme's, have gotten there, without her moving. Furthermore, how did they get her out, if she wasn't walking? What we have here is a "razzle-dazzle", people."

Aodhfin looked at the Elf with a raised eyebrow.

Varthstone lowered his eyes to the floor and shook his head. "How did they ever put you in charge?" he asked, before answering Aodhfin's silent query. "Overload the senses with the blatantly obvious," he said, pointing to the handprints, the knife, and the copious amounts of blood. "Your mind immediately assigns guilt. Esme at the scene, handprints match hers. Factor in a loud argument, and you have a crime of passion. Add to it a haunting and you reduce any suspicion by eliminating a follow-up after the initial inspection. Razzle the senses. Dazzle the mind," he said in finality, folding his arms.

"So...," Sange began.

"He's saying that Esme's been framed," Aodhfin said in understanding. "And the real killer is still out there."

THE GLYPH

Aodhfin took the news in stride. The killer is still at large, he echoed to himself. They executed the wrong person! Esme was innocent. No wonder she was haunting the manor.

Flexing his lacerated hand, he walked over to the fireplace to think. He was careful not to touch anything at the scene, or risk contaminating it worse than it already was.

He watched as Varthstone hiked up his robes so he could get closer to the floor to analyze how Gallach might have fallen, which position he might have lain that would explain why so much blood had gotten everywhere.

Sange fell back towards the entrance, and Aodhfin could tell she looked pale. While the large woman may not run from any battle, the sight of such a brutal murder unsettled her.

As Aodhfin turned once more to evaluate the scene, a strange glimmer caught his eye. He followed it. It was the mantle above the fireplace, or more accurately a vase.

The purist leaned forward and examined the porcelain container. It was lavender in color and looked to have held a bouquet of flowers. The lilies that had been within were now all curled and dead. There was something unusual about them though. The desiccated petals had markings on them.

"Varthstone," Bray called, still studying the strange symbols.

He felt the presence of Lotul as the sorcerer came up beside him, a curtain of blonde hair separated his face from Bray's. "What is it?"

Aodhfin pointed.

He watched as the Elf leaned forward, studying the vase, and then his eyes went wide in shock. He looked over to Bray. "Do you know what this is?" he said with a smile.

Bray shook his head no. That was why he had a sorcerer there, after all. "These are glyphs," he said in a burble. "The ones on the petals are sound-based, they pick up ambient noise. The shimmering one on the vase though, it's ocular."

"What does that mean?" the purist asked with a shrug.

The Elf's clean face was almost jubilant. "It means that someone out there witnessed the murder. It means that someone in this town is a sorcerer. And that, Ser, is someone I can find."

~ ~ ~

They knew they had to wait until the next day before they could move again. So, the trio retreated to the inn where Aodhfin had cleaned and stitched his wound, and caught a few hours rest. When he had awoken, he felt refreshed in body, but not in mind. Aodhfin was troubled. He was troubled at the possible implications of what they'd discovered inside the manor. Men of faith were committing terrible sins within Sentinel's Barrow. Men that he had respected. A bishop, an adjutant...

Aodhfin may have been naïve to the touch of a woman, but he knew what he had seen in that bedroom. It had been designed for one purpose, and one purpose alone. Sex.

It went against all that Aodhfin had believed purists to be: men of sanctity, men of the Maker. Yes, he understood the necessity of procreation, and that it was an enjoyable act. Nevertheless, the bed had all but been a shrine. Sex had become an instrument of Gallach's faith, and that should not be.

When he met later with the exactors, he shook himself of the demons of doubt that plagued him. He needed to find out what was happening in this town. He needed to find the errant killer. The smug smile on the sorcerer's face told Bray that the next step was going to be easy.

"I've got him," Varthstone said as Bray approached.

"You've been out already this morning?" Aodhfin asked.

The Elf shook his head no. Instead, he held up one of the dead lilies he had taken from the vase. "I counter-scryed the glyph. He tried to use it this morning, and I've got him."

Bray had no idea what the sorcerer was talking about, but if it led them to the witness, then that was good enough for him. "Who is it?"

Sange spoke up. "I **have** been out fer the sorcerer doin' a wee bit o' scoutin'. Turns out, there issin' Al-key-mist."

"Alchemist" Varthstone corrected.

"What I said," Sange countered, before continuing. "Alchemist in town that's good wit' flowers. An Elf whose name we already know."

"Fem Fonzil?" Bray asked.

The Elf nodded. "Turns out our mortician multitasks, and dabbles in a little sorcery too."

"He also has help. We saw 'er from afar day we arrived. When ye was speakin' wit Murrough," Sange added.

Bray nodded. "I remember. Black hair. She was tending a garden."

"And a direct line to Murrough," Sange added. "Perhaps a lion-son?"

"Liaison," Varthstone corrected again.

"Quit it," Sange snapped.

Bray grimaced. He didn't like to implicate the adjutant. "What is his motive though?" the purist asked. "Though I am loath to admit it, the Bishop has more to gain than anyone else from Gallach's death, save their daughter. Murrough though..."

"Don't rule him out because he's one of you," Varthstone said matter-of-factly.

Heat rose to Bray's face. Anger bit into his every word. "We have a chain of command here, exactor. Remember your place."

Sange put a comforting hand on his forearm. "Lotul is only statin' what we're all thinkin'. Dunna take it out on him," she replied to Bray softly.

Aodhfin nodded and stowed his frustration. He knew Sange was right. He had been thinking the very same since the night before. "Let's just go speak with our mortician friend."

An hour later, they were in the foyer of a funeral home. Soft golden wooden walls seemed to encase the trio gently. A smell of incense burned lightly in the air. Fem Fonzil sat before them, his long pale fingers interlaced on top of the table they all shared. Four cups of tea sat between them all, none of them touched.

Like Lotul, Fem Fonzil was a pale Elf with almond shaped blue eyes and dark blonde hair. Unlike the sorcerer though, he kept that hair cut short, so the pointed tips of his ears were clearly visible. The mortician wore dark pantaloons and a pressed grey shirt, whose sleeves were rolled up to his elbows.

Bray thought he was going to have to strong-arm Fem Fonzil into talking. He couldn't have been more wrong.

Tears lined the mortician's blue eyes. "Yes, they were my glyphs," he answered honestly. "I arranged them there about three months ago."

"Why?" Bray asked.

"I had to know who else."

"Whaddya mean?" Sange asked him.

His watery eyes looked at them all. Bray saw a bit of surprise in his eyes. "Bishop… Simonis didn't tell you?"

Aodhfin shook his head no.

Fem Fonzil buried his face in his hands, "Maker help me," the Elf sniffed once and looked back up at them, forcing his tears to stop. "Esme and I were intimate."

The news came as a shock to Bray,and he blinked several times in confusion. Yet when he looked at his exactors, they didn't seem at all surprised. Just how naïve was he?

Fem Fonzil continued, "We began having an affair about eighteen winters ago."

"Wait," Varthstone interrupted. "I'm sorry but I have to ask, how old was Esme?"

"Forty-winters-old," he said wistfully. "She was a timeless beauty. The Maker had truly blessed her, and cursed her."

"Go on," Bray told the mortician.

"When we first met, I knew immediately that Esme was a lustful woman who wasn't receiving the satisfaction a lady like her required. When Gallach left on a crusade, I politely interjected myself into her life," he said with a tight smile. "She did not oppose it."

Fem Fonzil looked forlornly out the window towards the Gallach Manor. "She was not happy with her place with Gallach, but the Jasian Enclave forbids divorce from a member of the clergy. To do so is tantamount to death. Gallach was no fool. He realized his beautiful bride was unhappy, and so he lavished her with treasures the best he could. They did not please him, as it was not his station, but he had hoped to win her heart with material trinkets.

"It didn't work of course. Her heart required more than material love, and her body deserved more than passionless intercourse," Fem Fonzil shook his head. "I did not hate Vey Gallach, but I was jealous that he was able to keep his wife, while I had to be an Elf of the shadows."

"Did ye kill 'im'?" Sange asked.

His blue eyes went wide. "Maker no!"

"What happened to change your position with Esme?" Lotul interrupted Sange's blunt remark. "Why did she cut you off after almost two decades of adultery?"

Fem's eyes darted to the other High Elf. "It was her daughter. She had just turned her back on the Enclave and renounced the Maker. Secretly, Esme was proud of Daria. She did not want her daughter to have to walk in the same footsteps as she, marrying a man she didn't love, and living a life she didn't want. I thought it an opportunity."

He looked back to Bray. "I asked her to leave with me. Return to the High Province. I thought she might take strength, like her daughter had shown."

"She refused you," Aodhfin said.

Fem Fonzil nodded, tears welling back up in his red, swollen eyes. "She said I had become too attached, and she broke it off."

"So being the florist as well, you sent those flowers to see if she became involved with another?" Varthstone asked. Fem Fonzil nodded and Bray could see fury replace the heartbreak.

"Who was it?" Bray asked.

Those now cold eyes looked at him, "The correct question to ask is who wasn't it?"

Bray and Sange stiffened. "What do you mean?" the purist asked.

Fem Fonzil scoffed, "I had been living a lie, thinking I was the only one that had caught her interests. It was why I said she was cursed. Esme had a lusting that was insatiable. She was hungry, always hungry, and I don't mean for food. I had thought myself to be feeding that need well, but I was wrong. She sampled from more than just I."

"Murrough?" Varthstone asked, and Bray winced.

To his surprise, Fem Fonzil nodded. "Simonis, too."

Dismayed, Aodhfin pointed a finger at the mortician and growled. "Don't defile their names with slander and accusations."

Fem Fonzil stared at him in shock.

Sange once more tried to talk him down. "Bray, we knew dis was a possibility. We talked about dis."

Aodhfin shook his head, a hot fury building in his heart. "Not this! I accepted that perhaps Simonis was trying to acquire material wealth, take advantage of a situation where he could push out someone who turned their back on the Maker, but not this. Adultery? Murder?"

Aodhfin lunged over the table and grabbed Fem Fonzil's tunic. "I want proof!"

Sange grabbed his shoulders and pulled him back, as Varthstone stood and moved around the table to separate the purist from the mortician.

Sange got them apart, and Fem Fonzil looked at Bray with a combination of anxiety and outrage. "Fine, purist, you want proof, you shall have it. You can have all of it!"

ONLY HUMAN

They stood before a strange round table about the size of a dining table for a family of four. At the outskirts of the table a series of glyphs, similar to what he saw on the vase, danced and glittered. In the center was a circular piece of reflecting glass. Aodhfin knew that reflecting glass was very expensive, so this bizarre bauble must have cost the mortician a small fortune.

What troubled Aodhfin wasn't the expense of the table, but what was within. It was bizarre looking into the glass and expecting to see your own reflection, but instead looking into another room completely. It was like peeking through a window into someone's house to spy on them, yet Bray wasn't seeing into the room now, but looking at the past.

Bray watched, to his revulsion, as a series of suitors came calling on the beautiful woman Esme, each set upon sating her carnal desires. They left thinking themselves triumphant, yet Aodhfin could see that wasn't the case. There was not enough for the woman before him. She was hungry, ravenous for her desires. It was beyond excess. In some instances, he witnessed her having multiple suitors in a single day, some only minutes apart. She had become an expert at it, hiding it from Gallach, and everyone else in town. As Fem Fonzil had been, each man had thought him her only affair.

Then he saw what revolted him most. The bishop. She took him on, like all the others, and his obese frame answered in kind. The sight made him sick to his stomach. Not because it was an elderly fat man getting off on a beautiful woman, but because this man was the voice of the Maker. His decrees were as if the Maker spoke directly. To watch this... defilement... of everything Aodhfin believed in, brought a bitter taste to his mouth, and rolled his guts in anger and sorrow.

"We're only human," Sange said to Aodhfin as she put her strong hand on his shoulder. Clearly, she could see the disgust and bewilderment written across his face.

"I've seen enough," Bray snapped harshly. "Show me the murder."

Fem Fonzil looked at him, and Bray saw the pain in his eyes for having to watch what his beloved did behind his back time after time. The purist wondered how it felt for the Elf in front of him, each time he watched. Like a wicked wound torn open repeatedly.

Fem Fonzil made some form of incantation with his fingers, and one of the glyphs began to shimmer brighter than the rest. The image was different now. The back of a man entered into view, the circle within a circle emblazoned upon his tabard clear to them, the plume of a feather sticking from his cap. Aodhfin seethed at the man… Murrough.

The adjutant began to disarm himself, first removing a gem-encrusted dagger and setting it down, and then his sword. Aodhfin hadn't noticed on their meeting the amount of frivolities he kept upon him. It should have been a sign! He should have known!

Before the man could take off his tabard there was a loud bang, and an older well-built man entered holding a cudgel.

Though in the twilight winters of his life he still bore a broad chest and keen eyes, Aodhfin recognized him from the portraits: Vey Gallach.

He swung the cudgel, striking Murrough across the back. The man moaned and tumbled, knocking over the chaise. Gallach did not relent, slamming the weapon repeatedly into his shoulders, chest, and back. They could hear him yelling 'betrayer!' and 'sinner!' repeatedly at the man. Finally Murrough relented to the elder, picked up his sword and fled.

Gallach wheeled on his wife, and to Aodhfin's surprise, he began to cry. Esme, however, seemed cold to his emotion, aloof. She stood up, walked over to the elder man, and slapped him hard in the face.

Sange gasped.

Gallach was equally surprised. His tears were replaced with a righteous rage. He grabbed Esme by the shoulders and began shaking her violently, screaming at her for why she had continued to betray him.

A sultry smiled played about her lips, and as he continued to get worked up in fury, she began to undo her chemise. Gallach saw this in alarm, and Aodhfin was baffled as well.

She was becoming aroused by his anger. She tried to pull him to the bed, tried to win him over with her natural charms, but Gallach was too far gone. He pulled away from her. They all heard him clearly say. "It's over, Esme."

She shot off the bed and apologized to him profusely, but he was shaking his head. "I cannot live like this anymore," he explained. "I've lost everything trying to help you. I've sacrificed everything. Even our own daughter resents what we have become. I will not lose my sanity over this as well. I'm sorry my love, but I must cast you out."

Esme dropped to her knees at his side, now crying and begging forgiveness. Pleading that there was something wrong with her, that she was broken, and he, like the Maker, should forgive her of her sins. However, Gallach was done; the purist could see it all over his face.

Gallach went to leave, when in desperation, Esme lunged for the dagger that Murrough had left behind. She drew the weapon on Gallach, and he looked upon her with pity. Esme stood and flanked him, moving to block his escape. Her back was to the glyph now, so that all they could see was the corner of her crème white shoulder and the long flowing raven black hair. The image faded for a moment.

"What was that?" Bray asked.

Fem Fonzil shook his head, "It's nothing. It happens now and again. I could show you countless other images that I have in regards to this where it has happened. Sometimes if someone close has magical prowess or a magical trinket themselves, it causes a momentary disruption in the scrying. It will come back, and unfortunately you will not miss a thing."

And indeed the image did reappear, just as Esme lunged at Gallach. The older man's eyes were wide with terror, which Aodhfin had found odd considering this was a man who had seen the horrors of war for decades. His attempts to block the dagger were feeble, and Esme's skill and deftness for striking at major arteries were definitely visible.

She plunged the weapon into his right thigh, and Gallach moaned in agony, but did little to stop her. She twisted the weapon and yanked it free, sidestepping the gout of blood that erupted with it, dousing the bed.

She then slid the dagger just under his armpit, erupting another major artery. Blood plumed, rich and vibrant down his yellow tunic, soaking it instantly.

Gallach dropped to his knees, his life's essence jetting out of him in sporadic pulses. He looked up glassy-eyed at the woman before him. Her back to the glyph, she rose the dagger high, and swiped down in a single fatal stroke.

The jugular severed on the elder's neck, a geyser of hot acrid spray splashed against the wall. He toppled over onto his side, blood hemorrhaging out of all of his wounds at an alarming rate. Esme turned to face the glyph and the image faded again.

They all sat mute, waiting for the image to come back. When it did, Esme was crawling back into the picture. She seemed confused. She crawled right into the blood and hefted herself by her hands up the chaise and onto the bed. When she turned around, Aodhfin watched as clarity set in. Esme screamed and dropped to the body. Her hands found the dagger on the floor, picked it up, and she screamed again.

Suddenly Murrough was there, bursting into the room. He stared at the scene, utterly dumbfounded. He began to yell at Esme to drop the weapon while she sobbed. The adjutant approached her slowly, his hands up in alarm. She turned and saw him, saw she was holding the knife and dropped it.

Esme looked at him, desperate and lost, and then as all the events seemed to come down on her at once, she fainted. Murrough managed to catch her before she hit the ground. He lifted her up and carried her from the scene, his feet never once encountering the blood.

They all sat still as they watched the life ebb away from Gallach, as the blood slowed to little more than a trickle and soak into the cherry wood floors.

~ ~ ~

"That's why he responded so quickly," Varthstone said, breaking the silence. "He was there when the murder took place."

Sange nodded and pointed out, "His dagger, too."

"But he is not an accomplice," Bray defended.

Varthstone raised an eyebrow. Aodhfin could tell he was going to retort, but quickly raised his hand. "This is not the place."

The Elf closed his mouth, stared at the Purist harshly for a moment and then nodded. Aodhfin turned to the mortician. "Were you watching this as it happened?" he demanded.

Fem Fonzil shook his head no. "Often I am not here to watch them at the time they are happening. Each glyph here can hold the information only once. Once it is disenchanted, it is gone."

"But you just showed it to us," Bray said.

Varthstone nodded. "But time is limited with a scrying glyph. It takes a spot on this table, and if one wants to scry again he needs to free a spot, rendering this vision abolished."

Bray understood. "You are not to destroy that vision, am I clear?"

The mortician nodded. "Yes, Purist."

"Does anyone else know about this? About your scrying?"

Fem Fonzil shook his head. "No one. Do you know what the bishop would do to me if they learned I had this! If the bishop learned there was a sorcerer even present in Sentinel's Barrow! Not even my apprentice, Nayria, knows about it."

"You are sure?" Bray asked.

The High Elf nodded. "Absolutely."

While Aodhfin wanted to say that Simonis was a Maker-fearing man, and no harm would come to Fem Fonzil for his indiscreet scrying, the purist wasn't so sure anymore.

"Is there any way to transfer that glyph?" Aodhfin asked.

Fem Fonzil shrugged. "Not that I'm aware of."

Aodhfin was going to press when Varthstone spoke up. "I hear that some of my other kin, Wild Elves in particular, are well-versed at scrying and transferring it. We High Elves, though, have no such means."

Bray sighed. Wild Elves secluded themselves from societies and he didn't know where any of their insular villages might be located within Gurgen. They preferred the large forested regions to the east, and Bray knew they didn't have that kind of time.

"We need to find Daria," he said.

"Or the will," Sange returned.

"Well… I might know where the will is," Fem Fonzil said as he began covering up the scrying table.

Everyone looked at the mortician. "Gallach was a pious man, and he spent most of his time at church praying."

"You think the bishop has it?" Bray asked.

Fem Fonzil shook his head. "Not that church," he returned. "Don't get me wrong, he was a man of the Enclave, have no doubt, but he was a solemn man, deeply introverted. He used the abandoned cathedral, the one for the old gods."

"How do you know all this?" Aodhfin asked as he scrutinized the Elf.

Fem Fonzil sighed as he put his face in his hands. He looked at them, forlorn. "You forget so soon that I was bedding his wife. You think I would not trace the steps of the husband?"

"Good point," Varthstone added.

A door closed behind them just as the mortician finished covering the table. Aodhfin was surprised to see it looked just like an alchemist's workstation now.

"Ah, Nayria!" Fem Fonzil said, suddenly jubilant.

Bray turned to look at the person entering and was momentarily taken aback. The young woman before him was simply exquisite. Long black hair encased her delicate and soft Elf-like features. She looked at them all with surprised green eyes that twinkled like gemstones. They were almond shaped just like an Elf's. She had a thin nose and full lips that demanded attention. He noted a very faint point at the tips of her ears. There was something strikingly familiar about her.

"You're a half-Elf," Varthstone remarked before Aodhfin could say anything.

"Yes," she said quietly. Then she directed her gaze to the mortician. "Ser Fonzil, I was unaware we had guests."

Fem smiled a genuine smile. "They were just leaving, dear apprentice." He looked at Bray. "The old church has wards crafted by your priests so that only a single key can gain access to it." He dropped his voice to a whisper. "It is likely it's there that he stored whatever was precious to him that he wanted to keep from anyone else."

Bray nodded. "Where do I find this key?"

Fem Fonzil's eyes glittered in a dark way and Bray knew he wasn't going to like what he heard next. "Gallach still has the key on him."

GRAVEYARD

"At least it's not as dark tonight," Sange remarked, looking at the bevy of stars in the sky.

Bray shook his head. "I can't believe I'm about to do this."

Varthstone smiled. "It is a very impure thing to do, isn't it?" The Elf leaned on his shovel as he looked at the uncomfortable purist.

Aodhfin Bray ignored the jibe and the trio walked quietly into the Enclave's graveyard. The small resting place for the deceased was located on the west end of town, nestled between the Enclave to the east, town housing to the north, and the old cathedral to the south. All to the west was the deep blue of Sowle Sea and the loud crashing of the surf.

The whole area was dank.

"You do realize when we start digging we are going to hit water fast. You know what water has likely done to Gallach's body over the last twenty plus days?" Varthstone continued.

Bray shook his head. "Let's try not to think about it, shall we?"

As they quietly walked into the graveyard, Aodhfin fell back to walk side by side with Varthstone. The Elf eyed him curiously, but Bray needed to know what the sorcerer knew about the manor. It had been troubling him all day. "You said we'd talk later about the haunting."

Lotul nodded, "I did."

After a short silence, Aodhfin shot him a look. The Elf sighed. "Okay. The house wasn't haunted."

"But… I saw Esme. She tried to throw me from a window!" he whispered harshly.

"We all saw something," Varthstone returned. "Each what we feared most at the time. That was the nature of the trap. It was very cunning."

"Trap?"

The Elf nodded. “An illusion trap, triggered to the doors on the second floor. I only figured it out after…,” he coughed nervously into his hand, “well, after my rather embarrassing episode of attacking the stairs.”

“What was your fear?” Bray asked. “And how did you figure out it was an illusion?”

Varthstone appeared momentarily skittish about revealing his fear, but finally he just chuckled and said, “I really hate clowns.”

“Clowns? Like jesters that paint their faces and do stupid things?”

Varthstone sighed and looked to the stars. “Yes,” he admitted. “They just… they really bother me.”

Aodhfin suppressed a laugh. “I can see that,” he agreed.

The Elf continued, “That’s how I knew it was an illusion. The sorcerer triggered the spell to react to our fears, and if you tell someone the manor is haunted, your fear will be… ”

“Ghosts,” Bray said.

“Naturally,” Varthstone replied. “Except I don’t fear ghosts. Part of my talents lie in dismissing spirits and poltergeists. So the illusion targeted what I was afraid of. Something that had nothing to do with an estate possessed full of vengeful spirits.”

“But she broke the window.”

Lotul shook his head. “You did. With your hammer. The illusion made you think it was her.”

Aodhfin still wasn’t sure. He had seen something before they opened the door, by the balustrades. Then when he had seen Esme’s spirit, she was wearing the same chemise as she had worn when she murdered Gallach. Bray hadn’t known that at the time. Still he picked out something important Lotul mentioned. “You said a sorcerer laid the trap.”

“Yes,” he replied, his hazel eyes sparkling. “And thus far we only have one in this town, don’t we?”

Bray bit his lip at he thought about it. Who had the most motive to kill Gallach? “Fem Fonzil.”

“The images we saw,” Varthstone continued. “They were altered.”

Bray shot him a look. “What?” he hissed.

“I didn’t want to say anything in front of the mortician and give away that I knew, but they most definitely were altered in some way. We need to find out why.”

Aodhfin thought on those words as they stopped behind Sange. She held a lantern down towards the tall grave marker. "Ere lay Adjutant Vey Gallach, a man o' war, a man o' the Maker," she said, reading his epitaph.

"Do you think Fem Fonzil lied about the key?" Aodhfin asked the sorcerer.

Lotul shrugged, "I suspect we will find out soon enough."

~ ~ ~

Between the three of them, they had the grave dug up in relatively quick order. Sweat and soil clung to him, making Bray's clothing feel like damp, soggy flesh. He was thigh deep in cold earthborn waters, and Sange, who was next to him, had ditched the shovel and was using her large hands to keep the running mud and clay at bay from sliding back into the hole.

"The casket is going to weigh a ton," Varthstone remarked. "Best to crack it and just remove the body."

"I'm not going to desecrate this man's final resting place any more than I have to!" Bray snapped. "This is bad enough as it is."

Lotul shrugged. "Have it your way, priest."

"All we have ta do is loosen it from da earth. Shoulda rise wit the water, right?" Sange asked.

"No," Varthstone commented from above them. "I took a look at the caskets while we were at the mortician's. Fem Fonzil weights them with stone so they will sink. I'm telling you, you'll need to remove the body."

Bray had a twisted feeling in his gut. "Well, Ser?" Sange asked. "What do ye wanna do?"

It was the first time in the last two days that she had respected his position, and Bray knew why. This decision was important to him. Detrimental to *him*, not them. She understood that, respected that. It gave him strength and an appreciation of the exactor at that moment.

"We crack the casket," Bray said finally. "We have to get that key."

~ ~ ~

Bray leveraged the shovel right between the slats, and Sange did likewise on the other side. "Ready?" he asked.

The woman nodded.

"Now!"

The two pulled their shovels with all their strength. Aodhfin saw deep grooves and valleys of muscles cut across Sange's forearm's and biceps. He was impressed in the details of her musculature. This was a woman who not afraid to be who she was.

It was against most of what the church stood for. Bray understood that. Ironic really, since the foundation of their faith was based on a woman's sacrifice. Still, Bray found himself respecting her usefulness.

Suddenly he felt a shudder in the handle of the shovel and it loosened considerably. A series of bubbles churned at the water they stood in, and then Bray felt something brush up against his legs.

A second later, a swollen body wrapped in cloth surfaced between the two of them. Bray looked down at it, confused, and then up to Sange. She had the same perplexed expression on her face.

He looked to the waterlogged body once more. It wasn't Gallach. In fact, it wasn't even human. Between the two of them floated a goat.

DECEPTION

"Is that a goat?" Varthstone asked, casting his lantern light into the hole.

"Yes it's a damn goat!" Bray growled.

Quickly, he pulled himself out of the hole. Sange followed. "We've been duped."

The sorcerer nodded. "Fem Fonzil."

Bray looked in the distance to where he knew the funeral home lay waiting. "It makes sense. Too much sense," he agreed. "Fem was angry. Not just with Gallach, but with Esme. She had deceived him, wronged him. He doesn't care about the will, or Gallach's possessions. He only cared that he loved her, and she used him."

"Then what are we waiting for?" Varthstone said darkly. "Let's bring him to justice!"

Bray nodded.

"Ugh... guys?" Sange interrupted. "I think we have a problem."

Sange pointed towards the entrance from where they had come. Standing there in the shadows cast by the gate was a lone, robed figure. A deep cowl covered their head, hiding their features. It stood there, watching them, unmoving.

"Fonzil?" Bray asked, reaching for the hammer at his waist.

Varthstone glowered at the lone figure. "I say we find out. Nothing I hate more than being made a fool."

Without waiting for Aodhfin's command, the sorcerer ran at the entity."Dammit, Lotul! No!" Aodhfin yelled after the Elf, but he did not turn around.

"What'n asshat," Sange remarked, drawing her axe in a single smooth motion from her back. "What do we do, Bray?"

"Flank it," Aodhfin answered immediately. "If it is a sorcerer, it will have a harder time with two separate targets."

Sange nodded and began to move left around the headstones. Bray went right.

Aodhfin kept his eyes on the unmoving figure as Varthstone ran towards it. When the sorcerer was only two dozen steps from the unknown person, it suddenly flared to life.

The cape flew open wide and three oblong objects scattered out with it. They took flight into the air, upon insect's wings, and it suddenly sounded like the graveyard was full of angry bees.

A small figure remained in the wake of the transformation. It raised a hand at the approaching Elf, and Aodhfin could only watch as the night turned to day before his eyes.

A huge fireball erupted directly in front of Lotul and, unable to slow his momentum, the unfortunate Elf vanished within the burning hot flames. There were no cries of pain, or screams of agony. Lotul was just… gone.

Aodhfin didn't have time to dwell on it as the three strange creatures flew their way. When they got closer to the separated duo, Aodhfin felt sick to his stomach at the sight of them. They looked like winged heads.

Aodhfin grabbed the shield off his back and rolled it forward with his free hand. In his peripheral vision, he could see Sange dropping her lantern and taking up her axe with both hands. The threat had just become very real.

They swept around the duo quickly, like hornets testing the range of their prey. Burning viridian flames flickered in place of their eyes and a series of barbed tendrils undulated beneath their wings like multiple stingers.

Aodhfin, no stranger to battle, kept his shield up and close to his chest, able to guard his exposed head if need be. He hadn't thought to wear his platemail in the graveyard this evening. He hadn't thought he'd need it. How wrong he'd been.

Sange swung her axe in tight, skilled strokes, trying to keep the winged monsters at bay. She did a good job keeping them back, but he knew the technique would wear her out quickly.

Aodhfin quickly looked back to where Varthstone had been. A large burning ball of fire stayed there, rolling in place. The small person, whom had been within the cloak, still stood by the gate, its features mute and indecipherable from this distance. Whoever they were, their focus was on the rippling globe of flames.

One of the creatures darted in at Bray. He raised his shield, deflecting a staggered series of blows from the stingers. A white pus-like substance dotted the surface of his shield, and it carried with it a pungent odor of decay. Like rotting vegetables.

Bray returned with his hammer, but the critter was too fast and easily avoided his blow.

Sange, across from him, was forced to fight two. She moved deftly for her size, maneuvering the woodsman's axe in a series of spins and twirls that he would have never thought possible from the weapon. It was like an extension of her being and she wielded it with the same finesse as a tigress used her own claws.

The winged beast moved in on Bray again, and this time the purist initiated the engagement. It came at him with a staccato-like attack, and as it swooped in, Bray swung out with his shield. It bashed the thing across its deformed face, crushing what looked like a nose and drawing black fluid from its mutilated orifice.

Sange too, cut a sharp arc with her axe, severing a wing from one of the things and causing it to spiral out of control until it collided into a headstone with a sickening crunch.

The beasts withdrew, and Bray saw from the corner of his eye that they had drawn the attention of the sorcerer. He had little time to call out to Sange before their assailer directed the ball of fire at them.

Aodhfin saw the ball roll at great speed towards the warrior woman. Before he could even second-guess himself, he sprinted towards her. Sange watched, stunned, as the rolling globe of fiery death tore her way.

Aodhfin gave everything he had to get to her, and had it not been for the fact that the sorcerer had to navigate the ball around grave markers, he would have never made it. As it was, he beat the undulating conflagration only half a breath before it hit. He slammed into the blaze, shield first, forcing the fire to explode in a series of sparks that washed up and over the duo. Aodhfin felt the bite of the fire against his forearm. He smelled the sizzle of his cooking flesh, and felt the tightening of his skin, but he willed the pain from his mind until the inferno had subsided.

In its wake, everything around him, including his shield, was blackened and marred.

Aodhfin glanced at Sange, who looked at him in awe for only a moment. He flashed a quick smile, but felt it melt from his face the moment her doe brown eyes changed from awe to horror.

Bray spun and raised his shield just as a series of stingers rained down on him.

His shield took the brunt of the blows, but a single barb slid through and grazed his arm. Immediately it became heavy and numb and Aodhfin saw, more than felt, his shield arm drop to his side and the shield tumble to the earth. He stared at his limp arm, baffled as to why it didn't function, when he felt Sange's strong grip pull him back.

More stingers lanced through the air, and Sange thrust Bray behind her as the two remaining creatures swarmed atop her. She swung and weaved the axe in a miraculous display of skill, but it wasn't enough to stop all of the lashing barbs from poking through.

Bray watched in horror as Sange was perforated over a dozen times, white fluid running from the holes in her leathers and skin. Her axe fell to the ground as she dropped to her knees.

Aodhfin came forward, swinging his hammer in wild strokes trying to keep the monsters at bay, keep them away from Sange. He smashed one across the side, collapsing its body inward, and it spun away wildly into the distance. He looked for the other when he felt a sudden piercing pain in his back. His war-hammer slid from his grip, and then he was falling. In the distance, he could see the shrouded figure walking away, triumphant.

Aodhfin and Sange were on their knees, bodies numb and uncontrollable. They were face to face, only a foot a part.

"Aodhfin," Sange mumbled, her voice slurred from the toxins running rampant through her body.

"Be brave," Bray whispered, his voice equally drawling.

The sound of the beating wings flared around them. An echo of death.

Her brown eyes blazed. "I'm not afraid," she slurred.

The flurry of sound stopped, and the purist knew that one of them was about to die. He tried to look for it but lacked the strength to see where it was. Sange stared fiercely into his eyes.

"Pray fer me, priest," she whispered, and Aodhfin could only watch helplessly as her head disappeared in a flurry of wings and tentacles.

REVEAL

Sange didn't scream.

Aodhfin began to pray aloud, his voice slurred and garbled, but he prayed. The mountainous woman's body writhed and twitched as the spurs drove themselves into her neck. The creature's whole body enshrouded her head, like a python devouring its prey.

Aodhfin continued to pray, growing louder even as his voice wavered. He tried to move, tried to fight the paralysis, but there was nothing. His limbs betrayed him. So he forced himself to watch. He would honor her. He prayed so she could hear him, all the way until her last moments, and he continued to pray even as her body stopped thrashing and fell still.

The tentacles pushed deeper into her flesh, and then Aodhfin heard a loud pop. Violently the creature pulled free, and Sange collapsed to the side.

Her head was gone.

The prayer left his lips. Bray still couldn't move.

Fear, oppressive and heavy, like water-laden armor, weighed upon him. A set of menacing eyes looked at him victoriously. They wracked his body with terror as they came closer, eyes that burned with an unholy green flame.

Bray wanted to raise his shield in defense. He wanted to pray to the Maker for his chosen deity's courage and blessings. He wanted to run. But he couldn't.

Paralyzed, and with all-consuming dread, he watched, helpless as it drifted towards him. A revolting, distorted head, suspended from insect-like wings. Around its ominous gaze was a crown of writhing tentacles all capped with wicked, barbed spines. Bray could see a pus-like fluid oozing from each of the dozen or so spurs.

The monster's mouth opened. He heard a loud pop and watched in disbelief as its jaws distended wide enough that it could enclose its maw completely around his own head.

Jagged teeth slavered at the impending kill, and Aodhfin Bray knew without a doubt that he was doomed.

Therefore, he did the only thing he could. He closed his eyes and tried to tell himself to be as brave as Sange had.

He waited to feel the pain thrust into his neck. He waited to feel the weight of the hideous beast close around his head. He waited to die.

The fluttering wings resonated in his ears like the beating of a hundred drums. It was a thunderous boom as it closed in on him. He knew the moment was upon him. His only regret out of all of this was that he never had a chance to tell Simonis about his son.

Even though the bishop was clearly a dishonest and immoral man, Bray wasn't. He should have told the man about his son. He had deserved to know. Now it was something that could never be.

He felt pressure then, but no pain. Surprisingly it was cold, as if the temperature around him had suddenly dropped. It was not something he had expected from a creature whose eyes emanated green flames.

Then he heard a thud, and felt something press against his numb thighs. Bray opened his eyes.

The creature lay there, against him, a lance of ice almost a foot long protruding completely through its head.

Confused, Bray looked up into the night. There, swaying, disorientated, through the forest of tombstones, steam rolling from his blackened robes, was Varthstone.

The sorcerer collapsed next to him, and immediately Aodhfin could see that some of the burns were quite extensive. Angry red flesh lined his face, and most of his blonde hair had been burned away. Blisters were already beginning to form on the Elf's hands, making using them difficult.

"Can you move?" he asked, his voice hoarse.

"No."

"Sange?" Varthstone said as he moved towards her. Aodhfin could only watch as he stopped halfway. "Oh, Sange."

"You need to go after Fem Fonzil," Aodhfin told the exactor. "You need to stop this."

Varthstone shook his head. "Not without you," he commented. "My arrogance already cost us Sange. I won't be responsible for you, too."

Aodhfin shook his head. "Don't blame..."

Lotul raised his hand. "Not now."

Aodhfin felt pressure on his body as the sorcerer began to search his wounds. "I think I can draw the venom out of you," he told Bray. "But it is going to involve magic, and it is going to hurt. Do you trust me?"

"Do I have a choice?"

"Not really," the sorcerer commented.

"Then do it," Bray ordered.

Varthstone swayed to his feet, placed one hand on Bray's back and began to draw on the magic of Creation. At first, the purist felt nothing but a strange budding pressure inside of him, then it began to intensify. Soon he felt searing heat and began to feel his blood boil. Pain ignited within him like an explosion, ripping through every fiber of his being and into his soul.

Aodhfin Bray screamed.

~ ~ ~

Minutes later the duo staggered to the funeral home. Bray had his shield across his back, but his hammer was in hand. Every nerve ending in his body felt like it was on fire, but he could move, and right now, that was what he needed.

Aodhfin hammered into the door, taking it from its hinges. It fell to the ground with a loud thud. They were now past the point of discretion. They knew there was very little time.

They moved with purpose, clearing each room together before moving to the next. Finally, they entered the back room where the scrying table was.

"No, no, no!" Varthstone said as he came around the table.

Aodhfin could already see that the surface that had once shimmered with glyphs was flat and dull. "It's gone."

Lotul slammed his fist against the table, and then hissed in pain as one of his blisters ruptured. He looked up, defeated. "We're too late."

Aodhfin let out a deep breath. He reached up and rubbed the locket around his neck in thought. As he did he saw a momentary flicker behind Lotul's head. Bray tilted his head as he stared, and then he saw it again. A gleam.

"What?" Varthstone said.

Bray moved around the scrying table and to the back of the wall. He studied it for a moment until he saw the shine of a glyph against a portrait.

"You've got to be shitting me," Varthstone said.

"Can you use this?" Aodhfin asked, nodding to the table.

"Damn right I can," he replied with a smile.

~ ~ ~

Fem Fonzil looked up at them through the table. "Purist, if you are seeing this, then I am dead," he stated bluntly. "Don't bother looking for my body as I'm sure they've ditched it somewhere by now.

"The image I showed you was modified. I figured it out shortly after you left because the inconsistencies bothered me. I missed things the first time because I'd been appalled by what happened. What I am about to show you are the real events that transpired. Brace yourself."

The image faded for a moment and then once more they were looking into the master bedroom of Esme. Everything played out the same as before, with Murrough entering the room and then the two caught by Gallach. After the beating of Murrough, and Esme's pleading, she went for the dagger.

She drew it on the elder man. Her stance was hardly threatening, and she looked awkward and unaccustomed to holding the weapon. Very different from the woman Aodhfin had seen murdering Gallach in the image, hours before.

Gallach moved on her with the skill of a seasoned veteran. In a single, deft move, Gallach wrenched Esme's wrist and plucked the weapon from her hand.

"That's new," Varthstone remarked.

This time the image didn't fade, and now he knew why. The creatures from the graveyard suddenly appeared from underneath the glyph.

"The fireplace," Bray murmured.

They swarmed atop the engaged duo and stunned them each. Both people froze in place. The creatures then disappeared the same way they had appeared, and Murrough entered the room.

He was fast and efficient as he pulled the dagger from Gallach's hand, sheathed it, and then scooped up Esme and carried her away.

The two stared at the image as Gallach stood there, terror in his eyes. Finally, Esme walked back into the room holding the dagger in her hands. Her back was to the glyph, but he recognized the chemise that she wore.

"This makes no damn sense," Varthstone whispered.

She straightened herself, adjusted her chemise once more, and fell into a combat stance that seemed far too natural to her compared to what they had seen seconds before. Esme lunged at Gallach. Apparently, the older man had gotten a little of his motor reflexes back, because he attempted to block the dagger. But it was too feeble, and Esme plunged the weapon skillfully into his right thigh. Gallach moaned in agony, but did little to stop her. She twisted the weapon and yanked it free, sidestepping the gout of blood that erupted with it.

The same slaughter they had seen before ensued, and then as Gallach lay bleeding out on the floor Esme turned to face the glyph, only it wasn't Esme, it was Nayria.

Aodhfin stared in shock. He now realized why she looked so familiar to him. Nayria looked like a younger, more slender version of Esme.

"Mother fu…," Varthstone said, fading.

She walked out of the room. Moments later Murrough came back into the image, holding Esme. He dropped her on the floor and left.

The rest played out the same, with Esme crawling into the blood, confused, tracking bloody handprints everywhere, and then screaming and dropping to the body. Murrough came in and arrested her.

The image faded back to Fem Fonzil.

"That's what really happened," he said bitterly. "Clearly I was wrong. Nayria *did* know about my glyphs, and she turned it to her advantage. She created a witness in me to prove Esme was guilty, just in case they needed it. Obviously until you came, they hadn't. Nayria knows I now know. I'm going to try to run, but I doubt I'll make it far, not with Murrough involved. I don't know why they did this, but you were right, the will is the key. You need to find it before they do. They never thought to look in the cathedral until I said something to you. I hope you had luck in retrieving the body of Gallach and that you now have the key. If I never see you again, good luck. And if I am dead, don't mourn for me. This has been a long time coming."

The image faded.

Varthstone looked up from the table to Bray. "Think he's being level?"

Bray shook his head. "I don't know. I still don't understand a reason here. Fonzil I get, Simonis I get, and Esme I even understand." He looked down at the reflective surface beneath them. "But Murrough?"

Aodhfin saw the patronizing look that Varthstone was giving him. "Give me a motive," he demanded and pointed to the table. "That was planned, Varthstone. Premeditated. I want to know why!"

Varthstone's expression changed. Slowly he shook his head. "I don't know why Murrough would be involved. We don't know him, don't know his history with Gallach. Perhaps he was like Fonzil, and found out he wasn't Esme's only lover."

Aodhfin grunted and waved a dismissive hand at the sorcerer.

"I'm trying to give you a reason, you stubborn son of a bitch," the Elf snapped. "This image is far more convincing to me than the last one we saw. If Fem Fonzil is lying, this one is a lot better than his last. If he's not, well he's now dead. So justice prevails there, eh? Nevertheless, you need to look past the fact that he's an adjutant, Bray. You are not infallible, you are human."

It was a hard reality for Aodhfin to face, but Sange had said almost the same words. They were only human. It was a similar realization as when he had watched Barodin die. The invincibility of youth had been lost in the wake of a dead friend. Perhaps it was time he shed his ignorance as well.

He acquiesced with a nod.

Varthstone clasped his shoulder gently. "I know it's not easy," he said with more empathy than the Elf had used in the past. "Now there is only the matter of getting into that abandoned church. If there are truly the wards Fonzil spoke of, then we still need a key."

A key.

A thought began to swirl in Aodhfin's mind. When they had needed to breach buildings before on the field of battle they had used a gnomish device called a 'master key'. It would propel a concentrated charge into a door, breaking locks and destroying barricades.

"Could you create a key, or tear down the wards?" Aodhfin asked.

The sorcerer shook his head. "That's not really my forte," he admitted.

Aodhfin nodded. He found his fingers on the locket, stroking the hasp that kept it shut. Even though locked, he knew with the right amount of force he could open it, even crack it if he wanted.

"I have a plan," the Purist said.

"A plan?" Lotul replied. "That fast."

Aodhfin shrugged, "More like part of a plan."

Varthstone crossed his arms. "Well then let's hear it."

Aodhfin explained.

MASTER KEY

Varthstone held up the rolled up piece of parchment in his hands. "This is crazy, you know that?"

"Will it work though?" Aodhfin asked.

The sorcerer grinned. "Oh, it'll work all right."

"Good, then we both have jobs to do. Good luck," Bray said.

Varthstone nodded as they left the funeral home. "You too, Bray. Be careful, and don't die."

With that, the sorcerer ran off into the night and towards the docks. Aodhfin knew they were thin on time, and he only hoped he wasn't going to be too late. He headed back to the graveyard.

When he arrived it didn't take him long to search for what he was after. He picked up the grotesque creature and examined it quickly. Underneath the strange disembodied head, he found two thick, leathery sacs. When he squeezed one he watched some of the stingers emit the white fluid. Carefully, he cut away one of the sacs and the attached tendrils. Very gingerly, he put it in his medical sack. He then looked up at the old cathedral.

This close to it, the ancient edifice looked imposing. It wasn't often that a church of the old gods remained intact. Most were torn down when the five-spired cathedrals of the Enclave were constructed. Gallach must have fought to keep it from sharing a similar fate.

Just inside, he could see the dancing light of torches, and he knew that it must be Nayria and Murrough. Now he needed to give them the sign.

Aodhfin searched Sange and found her flask of oil and flint. It need not be big, Aodhfin knew, but he wanted to make a statement. He dumped the entire flask on the front of his shield and struck the flint against the metal. Immediately the entire face of the shield erupted into flames. He shouldered the burning barrier and waved it high above his head.

Aodhfin looked out into the Sowle Sea and saw a returning glint of light. The purist drew his hammer and looked down once more at the remains of Sange. "I think you would have loved this. This is for you, girl," he whispered, and he charged the church.

~ ~ ~

A hundred feet from the towering double doors of the antique structure, Bray heard the sweet sound of thunder in the night.

A series of three booms all back to back. It was about to storm. It wasn't nature that was calling, but the Maker. Aodhfin had his master key.

A shrill whistle cut through the air as Aodhfin caught the quickest glimpse of it tearing through the darkness. It struck the side of the age-old building, rocking its very foundation, and tearing a massive hole through brick and wood.

The second whistle hissed by and Aodhfin saw as his key slammed into the earth, creating a two-foot-wide divot, and then bounced into the double doors. The primordial wood shattered under the might of the cannonball, tearing one down completely and swinging the other wide.

The third ball slammed through one of the stained glass windows and caused untold damages within. Phase one complete. He only hoped that Varthstone was on the move, because now it was Bray's turn.

Aodhfin charged into the church, launching over the broken timber easily. His flaming shield lit his way, but he knew that it wouldn't last much longer. That was fine. His message was delivered.

The inside of the church was a mess of vegetation. Between the cracks of the foundations, vines had found their way inside and thrived. He saw vermin skittering away, terrified to have their home disturbed after so long.

He had little time to admire the antediluvian architecture and instead searched for the murderers. He needed to find them and stop them before they got the will.

Bray pushed past debris and stone pews as he worked his way to the back chambers, and to the last place he had seen light. The west end. He made his way there.

The purist ducked under a deteriorating arch just as he heard the crunch of rubble. He spun just in time to see the flash of his firelight reflected off a silvery blade. He raised his shield, deflecting the blow and bringing him face to face with Adjutant Murrough.

~ ~ ~

"Who in the hells do you think you are?" the veteran growled as his blue eyes flared with hatred.

He pushed Bray back and moved forward in a series of concentrated stabs meant to drive Bray to ground. Aodhfin, however, had fought Wilders, and he was used to the overpowering might of their attacks. Murrough, in contrast, was a much smaller man.

The purist deflected all the attacks skillfully between his shield and the head of his hammer. He returned in kind with a low swing hoping to take out the adjutant's knee. Murrough narrowly avoided the attack.

"Not bad, boy," he commented dryly as he came in high with another series of tightly-controlled swings, forcing Aodhfin to be on the defensive. "But I have time and experience on you."

Bray didn't answer as he deflected the incoming attacks. He let Murrough get close before he suddenly lashed forward with his shield, bashing the adjutant in his shoulder and causing the man to stumble backwards.

The impact took out the last of the fire in an explosion of sparks. The room grew dim, only illuminated by the starlight from outside.

Aodhfin felt his skin begin to tingle, and looked down at his arm in surprise as the hairs began to stand on end. He felt pressure building in the air around him. Knowing what was coming next, he dove into a roll just as a burst of light exploded behind him. He came up just in time to catch the brunt of the fulmination in his shield. Electricity discharged across his arms and drove through to the heels of his boots, chattering his teeth and stunning him. Aodhfin knew it could have been much worse though, had he not caught the bolt of lightning in his shield.

Nayria stepped into the starlight, looking every bit like Esme in the pale glow. He thought he understood then. "You're her daughter."

"Eldest daughter," the half-Elf hissed. "Illegitimate, of course."

Bray's fingers and toes were numb from the electrical current that had poured through his body. He knew if he moved he would be sluggish and easy game for both Murrough and Nayria, so he stalled. "But why?" he demanded.

"Because I was denied!" the woman hissed. "No one could know that I was Esme's love child, begotten out of marriage. It would destroy Gallach, and no one could have that!"

Bray glanced to his left and saw Murrough stalking in the shadows. Trying to flank him, Nayria continued. "Gallach was a hero back then, and when he went on one particularly lengthy crusade, my mother had a dalliance with an Elf. The result: me. Bishop Simonis managed to keep it all secret, saying that Esme was terribly sick and bedridden at the estate. There, he cared for her, and delivered me. I was taken away to be raised in an orphanage while my 'sister' lived a life of luxuries. Three winters ago I came back to find who my parents were, and I learned the truth!"

Bray nodded at Murrough. "From him?"

She scoffed at him. "I need only look in a mirror, purist."

Aodhfin felt his strength returning right as Murrough charged at him. He ducked the man's viscous slash and punched out with the shield, catching the man in the ribs as he passed.

Murrough grunted and tumbled past him, crashing into a stone pew.

Nayria lashed out with another arc of lightning. Bray raised his shield in defense, but was too slow; the bolt ripped the battered shield from his hand, stinging it viciously.

The sorceress stepped forward, her fingers extended at Bray, and he knew she had him. "Where is the will!" she demanded.

Aodhfin looked up at her, baffled. He then realized that they hadn't found it yet. Quickly his mind modified his plan."It's safe," he lied.

She came forward and gripped his throat. He felt the trickle of electricity dancing across her fingertips, biting into his neck. "I will kill you," she spat.

"And it won't bring you any closer to the will," he answered. "You are running out of time, Nayria. You have hours left before Simonis takes it all. Then where will you be? Same as before, an orphan with no family."

Her green eyes were livid. "Oh I have family, purist," she remarked darkly. "And I think it's about time that you met them."

ENDGAME

Murrough regained composure quickly and took Aodhfin's weapon away from him. At sword point, he was forced to follow Nayria down into the catacombs. She grabbed a torch off the sconce and led him through a series of passages. As she did, she continued explaining how she learned of her patronage.

"When I arrived, that slime, Bishop Simonis, immediately became infatuated with me. I was naïve and childish, and had dreams of finding parents that loved me. In return for... favors." Bray watched her gag, revolted at the memory. "He told me the truth about Esme. It was a hope beyond my wildest dreams."

Bray could hear the longing in her voice, but watched as her face turned twisted and dark. "I approached her, her long lost daughter, and what did she do? Rejected me!" she spat. "Cursed me, told me I was a liar, and a sinner, and a foul creation and to get out of her life and never return! My mother!" she laughed bitterly.

"I tried everything to make her love me, but all she ever loved, all she ever needed, was the infatuations of men." Her eyes were cold and ruthless, just as Aodhfin had seen Esme's in the image when she had slapped Gallach. "I even tried blackmail, but she had the backing of Simonis, and he quashed that, threatening to have me tattooed and branded for having intercourse out of wedlock. The monster."

"I was lost, until Murrough found me," she said, glancing back to the man. "He knew of Fem Fonzil and his dalliance with Esme. He knew the Elf was a sorcerer. He conspired to have the mortician train me in the art of **Creation**."

"Why?" Bray blurted. "What was in this for you? An adjutant of the Maker! How could you?"

Murrough looked at him, his blue eyes so dark they seemed indigo. "The Maker," he spat. "This life has taken everything from me. My wants and desires. My hopes and dreams. The woman I wanted to be with was too lowborn for a purist, so they sent me here, leagues away from her where she could marry someone of rightful station. Then they shipped me a rightful bride." He scoffed. "A sow of a woman who was so bitter she could make milk curdle. She wanted nothing to do with me. She didn't even try to love me. Instead, she demanded that I care for her like Gallach 'cared' for his wife.

"I cared for her alright." The way he said it left no room for interpretation.

"When I met Nayria I thought I had a chance for something real again. But even that was spit upon because she is lowborn. Well she won't be when she is declared living heir of Gallach, will she?"

Aodhfin could see Nayria's white teeth glistening in the torchlight. She held her head high as she walked him into a wide circular room.

"You'll never guess who I bumped into when we came to the cathedral this evening. Hiding here all this time. I should've thanked Fem Fonzil before I killed him."

Another one of the beasts was there and the sight of it made Aodhfin cringe. It hovered, green eyes alight with flame. Tentacles undulated in the air. All of its tentacles but one. He followed it down and stared wide-eyed at the slumped over form before him.

"This is my sister," the Half-Elf told him. "Say hello to Daria."

~ ~ ~

"Now this is how I see it," the dark-haired half-Elf said as she paced around Aodhfin. "A purist will never give in to torture, right? You'd resist until I had no choice but to kill you. It is your way, after all."

She turned away from him and walked up to the slumped-over woman. Nayria grabbed her by her shoulder-length brown hair and yanked her head back violently. Daria was only a young girl, perhaps fifteen winters at most.

Immediately one of the creature's spurs came around and stabbed into Daria's neck. The girl twitched. Aodhfin tried to lunge at them, but stopped when he felt the length of Murrough's sword at his throat.

"That is what I thought," Nayria said with a smile. "You will do anything to defend an innocent, won't you?"

Aodhfin glared at her, outraged. "You would kill her for... for wealth?"

Nayria nodded. "And love," she added, looking at Murrough. "The question is why will you let her die? What is in this for you, purist? The murder has already been solved. No one questions it. Your job is done here. No one at the Citadel cares about Sentinel's Barrow. Why do you care who gets Gallach's wealth? I mean look at your choices: a corrupt bishop, a heretic who turned her back on the Maker, or an orphan. Really, is it such a hard decision?"

"When the orphan is a murdering psychopath, yes. Yes it is," Bray fired back.

Nayria's eyes darkened. "Funny. I didn't think purists had a sense of humor."

Another stinger slammed into Daria's neck and she started to gurgle.

"Oh. Look at that," Nayria said flatly.

Aodhfin took a deep breath, his body quivering in rage.

"The will," she demanded.

Bray tilted his head. "Have you checked Gallach?"

"His body was the first thing I eviscerated. There was so little of him left in the mortuary that I had to place a goat in the coffin to give it weight," she hissed. He had forgotten that she was the mortician's assistant.

Bray flinched as another spur buried into the girl. Daria let out a strained moan.

"I'll tell you what. I'll let you think on it, but don't think long." The tentacles rolled in Daria's neck causing her body to convulse. "The Vaus'Giel is impatient for its meal. The more impatient it gets, the harder it is to control."

Aodhfin knew he was out of time. He could see the Vaus'Giel's mouth slavering in anticipation, and he would not let Daria die. Nayria was correct in her assumption of his character, he couldn't abide it. He let his hand fall under his medical pouch.

"Okay," he said, hanging his head low.

Nayria's eyes widened in expectation. "Where?"

Aodhfin looked down and began to open the medical pouch with his other hand. Seeing this, Murrough knocked his hand out of the way and thrust his hand inside.

Bray squeezed the bottom of the pouch gently.

Instantly Murrough recoiled his hand, hissing in pain. His turned his hand over and he stared at his palm in shock. Four tiny perforations were on the pad, all oozing a white, pus-like fluid.

Aodhfin felt the sword at his neck droop, and he reacted.

He plucked the weapon from Murrough's hand easily, just as the Vaus'Giel dislodged itself from Daria. It came at him in a flurry. Prepared, Aodhfin swung the sword in perfect precision as it arced towards him, tentacles writhing.

Moving on its own momentum, the creature couldn't avoid Bray's attack. Its face exploded in a mist of black cruor as the sharp blade cleaved through flesh and bone, cutting it in half.

Nayria screamed in rage.

Aodhfin grabbed the paralyzed Murrough by the shoulder and spun the man in front of him just as the sorceress attacked.

Lightning cut through the air like a deadly knife. It lanced forward with lethal speed, headlong into the frozen adjutant.

The veteran grunted in pain as the fulguration hit him full bore, crashing through his chest and exploding out his back. The force of the attack knocked Bray back.

"No!" Nayria wailed in horror as her dead lover collapsed to the floor, a smoking fist-sized hole in his chest.

Aodhfin crinkled his nose at the scent of burned flesh. He moved on Nayria while she was still in shock, raising the borrowed weapon up to the sorceress' chest. "It's over."

Nayria spit at him, "I'd rather die! You'll nev..." She never had a chance to finish. Aodhfin turned the sword to the flat of its blade and backhanded her across the face with the weapon. He couldn't risk her casting any of her perfidious magic after all...

Nayria crumpled to the ground, unconscious.

~ ~ ~

An hour later, the local militia was escorting a bound and gagged Nayria out of the catacombs. Daria was now conscious, but groggy. She had taken a heavy dose of the Vaus'Giel's venom.

Varthstone made sure that she received care, while local healers doted on him as well.

Bray had to admit: the exactor had really come through. The Elf's task had been to conscript the captain of the ship they had sailed on to blow a hole in the cathedral. Sange's death sealed the deal.

Afterwards, he had to force Bishop Simonis to go to the funeral home where he would have to bear witness to the true nature of Adjutant Gallach's death via the scrying table. Judging by the swelling around the bishop's left eye, Aodhfin felt that Varthstone may have 'forced' a bit too hard. That was fine with him.

Aodhfin now found himself alone with Bishop Simonis. "I supposed congratulations are in order, Purist Grey," the thick-bodied man said condescendingly. "But I don't see why this couldn't have waited to be brought to my attention until the morning! You have everything under control here."

Aodhfin took a deep breath. It was all he could do to keep from striking the man. Instead, he pointed his finger into the obese man's chest. "You are partly responsible for all of this!" he growled at the bishop. "Your blatant disregard for the lives of those around you, whom you are supposed to serve, is a mockery to the very church you represent! You are a sinner, a tyrant, and a fraud. I just wanted to tell you this in person before I give my full accounting of what transpired here to Adjutant Daz."

"How dare you, Grey! You have no right to speak to a man of the Maker in such a way!" the Bishop bellowed.

Aodhfin grabbed the collar of the bishop's vestments and pulled him close. "It's Bray! And I have every right!" he hissed. "You abandoned the values of the Maker a long time ago, you piece of shite! If it weren't for my love of my friend Barodin, I would strike you down right now! It'd be doing this world a favor."

"Speaking of which...," Bray began. As much as he detested the man, he had a right to know. A right to know about the fate of his son. He let go of the bishop and unclasped the locket. He placed it in that elder's soft hand. "I regret to inform you that Purist Commander Barodin H. Simonis was killed in action defending the Citadel against insurgents on the third day of this season of greening."

For a moment, Bray thought his voice might fail him, that he wouldn't be able to convey the message, but it had not. Still the anguish of his own words poured from him. The persistent hopefulness of his human heart had refused to let him accept the intuitive certainty of his friend's death. He had been there after all. He had seen it. Now, though, in conveying it to the bastard before him, the reality came down hard.

He felt his own eyes watering.

The bishop looked down at the locket. "My son is dead?" he whispered.

Bray nodded.

For the first time, the bishop appeared human to him, weak, as his face turned purple in what Aodhfin knew was an inescapable sorrow filling every part of him. "But why the locket?" Simonis asked, his voice faint.

"I don't know," Aodhfin admitted. "Adjutant Daz gave it to me before I set sail for Sentinel's Barrow. I had assumed it was a personal article of Barodin's for you."

"Actually it belonged to my father," a wisp of a woman's voice said between the two.

Aodhfin looked down to see the rundown frame of Daria standing near them. "May I?" she asked holding out a shaky hand.

Simonis, lost in grief, didn't even recognize that he was handing the locket to a heretic. He dropped it in her hand absently.

Aodhfin, who had been tempted to open the locket repeatedly, watched as Daria reached down and deftly undid the latch on the side. When she opened it up, he saw clearly the drawn likenesses of Daria and Esme inside.

Then Daria did something most curious. She turned the locket over and slammed it between her palms. Suddenly the little drawing popped out and Aodhfin could see it was part of a larger piece of parchment, meticulously folded.

"When my father was killed, I knew immediately that it had not been my mother. Still, Murrough closed the case and executed my mother before anyone would even begin to investigate. I knew no one here would listen to a girl who had turned from the Maker, over an adjutant who had witnessed the whole 'murder'. I needed an outsider. So, I sent this locket along with a note to my father's old friend, Adjutant Daz, pleading for aide. I also knew that whoever killed my parents must be after their wealth, and that I was the only connection to that wealth, minus the will. So I hid where I knew no one would care to look and I put the will in the safest hands I knew of."

She unfolded the parchment repeatedly until it was almost the size of her hands. Aodhfin could clearly read the very first line: 'The last will and testament of Vey Gallach'.

She smiled up at him. “The hands of a purist.”

Aodhfin couldn’t help it; he began to laugh.

EPILOGUE

Adjutant Daz looked over his desk at Purist Bray with concerned eyes. "I had no idea the malfeasance ran so deeply."

Bray nodded. He had just finished explaining in full detail his accounting of the Sentinel's Barrow murders.

Suirokirt Daz took a deep breath and placed the written report on his desk. "You did a fine job, Aodhfin. I didn't mean to make your first command so perplexing, but you handled it well, very well."

"Thank you, Ser," Bray said.

"I hope you now understand why I assigned Exactors instead of Purists for this case?"

Bray nodded. "You needed impartial parties. Too many Purists, and we would have sided with the Church without question."

The adjutant nodded. "You have a sharp wit Aodhfin, and an open mind when necessary. For that I am glad."

Daz slid another parchment across his desk. "In fact, you handled yourself so admirably against a sorceress that I think this next assignment should go to you."

Bray looked down at the words scrawled atop the docket, 'Ambrosia'.

"Do you feel up to it?" Daz asked.

Aodhfin nodded. "Yes, Ser."

"And how do you feel about magic, son?"

Aodhfin looked out of the office where he saw his exactor waiting. He turned his head and looked Daz in the eyes. "After what I've seen, after how I was manipulated by an illusion, after watching comrades die to beasts under a spell, I think it is perfidious and vile."

"I see," Daz said.

Aodhfin continued, "But I also think in the right hands, those tempered by the Maker, **Creation** can be a gift."

"And you think Exactor Varthstone is such a man?"

Bray nodded. "I think he can be, yes."

"Good to know."

"Your daughter, too," Aodhfin added quickly. He remembered that Daz's daughter is a gifted healer and didn't want to sound too disdainful towards magic users.

"Yes... my daughter," the adjutant replied absently at his words. Almost distantly.

Bray saw something peculiar in Daz's eyes, so he knew he should quickly change the subject. He looked down at the words before him once more. "I must admit that I found the betrayals in the church more troubling than any of the magic, Ser."

Aodhfin glanced up to see a tired look now in the adjutant's eyes. "The closer we are to the light, the darker a shadow we cast, my son. Temptations of the forbidden can be strong if not tempered by faith, friends, and family." He looked down sadly. "Sometimes we cast that shadow deeply onto the ones we love, instead. We suffocate them in a void so black, and we don't even realize we are doing it."

"Is that what happened with Esme?" he asked.

Daz shrugged. "I don't know," he answered and pinched the bridge of his nose. "Perhaps."

A long silence filled between them. Bray found himself waiting uncomfortably. Finally Aodhfin thought Daz was done speaking about it and was about to conclude their briefing when he suddenly continued. "Sometimes I think our struggles as men of the Maker push our women away from us. We lose sight of how precious they really are. How fragile our control on them is. Then they do something completely irrational, that makes no sense whatsoever, and forces us to realize the demons of our own ignorance. Like a cry for help that is heard far too late."

Aodhfin could see Daz's eyes watering as he looked out of the window of his office towards the monolithic spirals of the Citadel.

"You think Esme had made that cry once?"

"I think she made it many times, and they fell silent against our deaf ears."

His tone of voice, though, and his use of the word 'our' sounded very different to Aodhfin, as if it were more personal. "Ser, is something wrong?"

A tear broke away from Daz's dark eye and cut a swath down his rugged face. "My Carmella," he whispered.

Aodhfin felt his stomach drop and his body grow cold. “Your daughter,” he said quietly. ‘My Carmella’, echoed in his mind. His beautiful, radiant, intelligent, fifteen-winter-old girl. A young woman engaged to be wed to a purist she hadn’t seen in over a winter.

Daz’s eyes looked to Bray apologetically.

“She’s pregnant, Aodhfin.”

4853 E.o.E

TWO WINTERS PRIOR TO THE EVENTS OF STORMWIND

By:
J. P. Strohm

THE ATTACK

The loud explosion echoed in his ears just before he felt the concussion wave. It knocked him backwards head over heels at least twice. The debris of wood, glass, and stone peppered his entire armored body as flame erupted, engulfing the building before him and his contingent unit. He went flying over fifty feet, striking hard on his chest and stomach.

His body ached as he struggled to move. The dark brown leather armor seemed oppressively heavy. He couldn't make out the voices or screams of those around him. He shook his head, trying to remove the ringing within it and to clear up the muffled distortion. Slowly he moved his arms to a position to get up.

Everything was blurred. The blast definitely did its job. It disoriented not only his Jasian Enclave purists' contingent, but dozens of emerald and silver men of the Buckner Guard.

He managed a kneeling position, when a muffled yell rang out. Blurry individuals ran in every direction. Slight hints of color were the only thing he could make out here or there. Humanoid forms with emerald and silver were engaging grey looking silhouettes of other combatants. There were some hints of blue also fighting for their lives against the blurs. *The rebels,* he thought.

One ran up to him holding something with both hands. Was it a large pole? No. It was a two-handed battle axe. Just as he began to focus on the large hands holding the weapon, he felt a force cave in his chest, knocking him on his back. He saw stars. Air burst from his lungs repeatedly by the impacts delivered by the assailer's feet and the ground itself.

Instinct took over.

He quickly grasped at the ground, gathering up much of the loose dirt and debris and threw it upward at what he could make out as the silhouette's head. The attacker dropped the axe, flailing at where he had targeted.

Free of the onslaught from the ax-man, he rolled off to his right and stood up. His footing wasn't sure yet and he still stumbled a bit. He then drew his rapier and short sword. The sounds were getting clearer now, as he could hear the blurry form in front of him speak after spitting. "You're going to pay for that, heretic." He then saw it reaching down, picking up the shadow of the battle axe.

The image of the rebel before him was clearer now. This threat was dressed in a makeshift splint mail armor of various pieces. He was tall, five foot ten inches perhaps. He was no more than a commoner, a farmer maybe? It was obvious by how ungainly he handled the weapon. The rebel charged.

He reached up with the flat of his short sword and stopped the arc of the battle axe at the weapon's shaft near the blade attachment. With lightning speed, using his rapier, he slit both wrist areas just past the hands, then across the right cheek.

The enemy had no choice but to drop the weapon and stumble back two or three feet. The rebel took the now bloodied arms and covered his damaged cheek with his hands. He stood, dumbfounded, as the pain and the shock of what just happened sunk in. The rebel's dirty blonde hair whisked in the wind and blue eyes now stared at the nimble defender with anger.

Ignoring the rebel for a scant second, he noticed the tattered area now was becoming clearer. The travelers' inn on the outskirts of Westgate that he and his contingent were escorting His Eminence Ser Marodin Tarnis to was gone. It was nothing more than a heap of burning wood and rubble. Bodies lay strewn in all directions, some his contingent, some the Buckner guard, and of course others, innocent bystanders, including children.

More rebels were running to fight only to be cut down before they even knew what was happening. It was a mix of humans, Goldhym, and Gnomes, and they didn't discriminate against those they thought were in authority positions.

His focus came back to the rebel before him. He placed himself in a defensive stance with his left leg forward and right leg back, the blue tabard in front of his armor flowing in the wind. He flexed his five foot seven frame, shaking away the last of the kinks. His studded brown leather armor, with so many small knives it gave the armor a chain mail appearance, was quickly losing the burdening factor it had moments before.

He tensed himself, preparing for another attack. He placed his short sword to his right and slightly behind him, and in his left, the rapier, out in front diagonally across his chest. His black hair flowed in the wind, no longer held in its back pony tail straps. He squinted with hazel eyes at the adversary in front of him. "For the record, asshole, an attack on one of the bishops of the Jasian Enclave is penalty of death, no matter what god you serve."

The man stared, nonplussed.

"If I can disarm you at only a fraction of my capabilities, I would suggest you finish the job quickly, before I regain my full potential. If not than I shall send you to the abyss of the Defiler," he hissed before smirking at the rebel combatant.

"Very well, priest!" the rebel yelled back and looked to his left and right as other rebels gathered. The combatant nodded in the direction of the leather-armored warrior to signal the others to engage.

Three of them moved around trying to flank the holy warrior. The fourth, the wounded, cautiously moved forward with a small dagger to assist as needed.

He could make out the general features now, and could see more clearly the individuals in their armor holding weapons. They were all wearing splint mail, carrying smaller axes. Two were also holding short swords. He quickly surveyed his surroundings. The only way he was going to survive was going to be fighting his way out of the human gauntlet. He quickly moved left and right trying to give each combatant face time, waiting for one of them to make their move.

The one on the right moved first, attacking with the small axe and hoping to counter with the short sword. The others engaged right after, their weapons down toward him to inflict additional piercings upon his body. They tried to time a coordinated attack the best they could.

The religious warrior parried with his short sword, piercing the man on the right through the throat to the back of his neck with his rapier. Retracting the weapon quickly, he shifted on the balls of his feet on the scree, extending the rapier to the other targets, hitting various areas.

The rebel with the dagger he hit again in the biceps, disarming him once again. The combatant on the left he sliced the inside the right groin area. As for the one man behind him, he cut into the abdomen area of the armor, exposing the flesh. The priestly fighter tucked to his left, backwards rolling just above the man, who fell to the ground, clutching his groin. Standing back up, pointing his rapier at the two adversaries left standing, he then commanded, "Last chance. Surrender and maybe His Eminence will be more merciful than I."

"Screw you, priest!" the rebel screamed. He then, with his bloodied left hand, smacked down on his right forearm. There was a small cracking sound like glass breaking. A flash of light, a gust of wind, and the religious warrior was being forced backwards... again.

REGROUP

He awoke quickly and found himself lying on the floor in the common room of a small bakery. He was about to rise and reach for his weapons when a hand on his right shoulder steadied him. "Easy, Exactor Tyberius, we're safe for now," the large holy man above him dressed in plate mail armor said.

He was not taking his blue eyes off the windows or entrance of the small shelter they had acquired. Tyberius could hear the screams and sounds of battle outside, then the explosions in the distance.

Tyberius turned his head up and toward the door. "How many…?"

"We're down to thirty-five, most lost from the explosion at the inn," the sentry answered.

The leathered warrior slowly moved to one side and began to get up to a crouching position, looking for his weapons. The large man now on his left side handed them to him. "Here, exactor. Figured you may need these when you awoke."

Tyberius looked at his companion, who was the contingent's second in command, Ser Carlum Metteros. The hunched down man was taller than he at five-foot-eleven. His platemail was banged up and his mace bloodied. The exactor noticed that the kite shield he always bore was not with him.

Metteros, recognizing the look, answered. "Damn rebel sinners had me outnumbered. I took out three before I realized it was me or the shield." He smirked a bit. "I can always get another shield; it's just a possession. I won't need it when my time comes to meet the Maker."

The exactor looked around at the bakery. Most of the provisions were gone. Windows were smashed, and the main door was off the hinges but was still in an upright position, barricading the entrance. The kitchen was behind them. Next to that was a flight of stairs leading to the second story of the building.

Tyberius then noticed others of the contingent within the room, kitchen, and stairs. He counted at least twelve on this level, all crouching and ready for conflict. Some were missing shields. Others were using temporary weapons such as small knives, even forks they found in the bakery. Those with the small weapons were not far from the few veterans that still had their shields and maces. He counted only three veterans in all, not including, of course, Metteros.

"What of Ser Hardin and His Eminence?" the exactor asked.

"Ser Hardin was killed protecting His Most Holy. He took the main force of the blast. A plank went through his chest, stopping his heart. His Holiness is upstairs right now in meditation and prayer. He seeks direction from the Maker."

Tyberius shook his head. He couldn't believe the chaos going on outside. "We all heard the rumors of civil unrest here in Buckner. Is this the reason the bishop wanted to leave so quickly?"

"It's not Gurgen's problem. All bishops are recalled from the Fermania Territories back to the Citadel. The orders came directly from the Supreme Pontiff himself," Metteros replied, not looking at him but still looking outside.

The exactor stood up, alarming his fellow warriors who were already on edge from the battles taking place outside. Re-attaching his short sword and rapier belts onto his armor, he started checking knives on the armor. One of the warriors in the room called out, whispering, "Are you crazy! You're going to bring these insurgents upon us!"

Tyberius turned his head in the direction the whisper came from. He replied in a low voice, "So we are just going to leave quickly and quietly with our tails between our legs? Are we even going help any of the innocents caught in the crossfire? How is that the purist way?"

"And what do you know of the purist way, criminal cur?" a voice boomed from the stairs.

All the warriors immediately stood at attention and placed their right arms across their chests. They bowed slightly from the shoulders and lowered the heads and eyes to the ground.

The large man continued down the stairs. His ornate satin white robe with gold and silver trim didn't seem to have a speck of dirt or dust on it, even after the blast at the inn. Off to his left and right behind him were two young acolytes holding the trailing edges of the garment. They did this so it would not cause His Eminence to trip on the stairs. Surrounding them all were four purist warriors of the contingent, protecting the Holy Man and the young priests.

The bishop reached the bottom stairs, dismissed the acolytes, and let the guards fan out. The six foot tall man stood with the confidence of faith that allowed him to guide such rabble. His black hair was cut short at the shoulders. His piercing blue eyes scanned the room. "Stand down, my fellow warriors," he commanded.

They all obeyed.

His Eminence Ser Marodin Tarnis, the Bishop Missionary to Buckner, was ready to enlighten his contingent on what the Maker had told him in prayer.

THE MISSION

Tyberius didn't like the plan. But he followed his fellow comrades anyhow. Bishop Tarnis explained in a sermon format how they were to get away from Westgate. It was a simple plan: get to the nearest still-intact stable with horses and carriages and commandeer them to get back to Gurgen.
As for the inhabitants of Buckner's western town, he explained that because of all their sin and greed of the Seafarers Caucus' policies, the Maker would purge Buckner's greedy to show the realm of Kuldarr the righteous path.

As for any opposition they would encounter, he did a right of blessing to ordain all of them in the name of the Maker. He did the ritual with holy oil to ensure they would vanquish all those that stood in their way to get back to the holy city, The Citadel. It was during that ceremony Tyberius noticed the baker's family at the top of the stairs holding one another. They were trying to comfort each other for the horror that was coming.

When His Eminence came to anoint him with the oil, Tyberius held up his hand and politely declined. "Forgive me Most Holy, but I cannot accept the Maker's blessing. I am not worthy of this task before me. I must first seek repentance for my humanity in this matter. I request this blessing to be held for my final hour."

The bishop replied, "Very well, exactor. I will pray that this journey back to the Citadel will allow repentance for your sins and allow you to finally understand what it is that makes one pure before The Maker. Then when you accept the True Faith, you can be finally recognized as a true holy warrior." After he said that he lowered his hand for Tyberius to kiss the ring upon it. The exactor did as tradition and respect of position required.

They left the bakery in haste, and entered the debris filled streets. There was chaos from all the looting and destruction from the earlier attacks on the town. It looked like a cyclone had come through the area. The explosions had died down, and there seemed to be less screaming, for now.

Tyberius took that as the first wave was done and the second was not too far away. He figured the next series of attacks probably would happen at sunrise. That only gave them about four hours of darkness to work. This of course was if they didn't run into anyone that would stop them. They had to find one of the main stables near the main trade road exit of Westgate before their time expired.

After dodging in and out of buildings and alleyways for about an hour, they came around a corner and found an entire block utterly destroyed. Six buildings were reduced to burning rubble. In between the flickers of the fire light, refugees were gathering what they could and trying to make their way out of the battle-ravaged town and towards the safety of Buckner's Sea of Walls.

Metteros held up his fist, indicating for the group to hold. In the middle was Tarnis, the second in command, who then hand signaled to his exactors to move ahead and scout. Tyberius didn't know the other two well, nor did he ever converse with them in his off time. All he knew was one was a sorcerer, a High Elf, and the other a warrior type, human, and not the religious type. They, like him, had the skills that sometimes outmatched their contingent's brute force.

The three exactors made their way down the side of the street. Tyberius on the left, the Elf on the right, and the human fighter down the middle. Tyberius knew the drill, they were the bait so that the contingent could either attack, or as in this case, avoid detection.

The trio made it past the damaged block and to the small town square. More people of Westgate were hiding or trying to move within the shadows to safety, away from the chaos. Seeing no rebels, the fighter exactor then went back a little and gave the all clear signal back to Metteros. The contingent began moving up towards them. Tyberius caught a glimpse of something in between the buildings that were on fire, right when the unit was halfway toward them. It was a small gnomish woman dressed very strangely. She had a peculiar wood and stone staff. He knew at once what she was: a sorceress.

She tapped her staff on the ground three times and the ground erupted all around the purists. Four hidden golems, twelve feet tall, emerged from the debris and closed in on them, immediately attacking the group. The exactors ran forward to save their comrades. The elf began to engage the gnome in a magical fight. The fighter ran up to the first golem and started swinging. Tyberius entered the fray, attacking the same golem as the exactor fighter, assisting the contingent as much as he could.

The religious warriors did not fare well in the battle. The earthy golems were not of flesh and blood as most adversaries. One swipe of their long rocky and hardened dirt arms easily knocked an average of three of the warriors to the ground. Then the large rock-shaped foot would attempt to crush them while the fallen were prone. Weapons were useless. All the holy warriors could do was chip away at the mass of the monsters before them.

Tyberius saw the sorcerer exactor fall to the gnomish woman, but not before he noticed his comrade's attack had hurt her. The golems seemed to hesitate for the briefest of moments.

Tyberius capitalized on it. He dodged and weaved in between his fellow warriors and past the bishop to change targets. When Tyberius did so, it exposed an opening for one of the monsters to come closer into the group.

The creature swung its massive arms and knocked down three more warriors right in front of His Eminence, startling him. His scream was like that of a little girl, but he yelled at the passing rogue, "How dare you abandon your most holy!"

The exactor emerged from the mass of flailing, battling bodies no more than five feet from the little arcane attacker. She looked at him and smiled wickedly. He returned the smile and slightly bowed, but not before flinging a knife in mid-motion. Her smile quickly diminished as she felt the impact and looked down, seeing the weapon. By the time she lifted her head, Tyberius was in front of her and he could see the pain in her eyes from his fatal blow.

As he removed the rapier from the head of the little woman, the golems all fell to the ground with a loud thud. He turned to group, now down to twenty-three. Eight were injured, badly. He looked at the bishop with malcontent and anger. "How many more will have to die just to save your hide, all in the name of the Maker?"

The others within the contingent stood in shock at the man defying their bishop. The six-foot man wearing now a bloodied and dirty ornate satin white robe grabbed Ser Metteros next to him and forced him out of the ranks and in front of Tyberius. "Contain your exactor! How dare he even address me in belligerent disregard to his station and place! You know the punishment!"

Metteros approached the exactor. As he got within a few feet, Tyberius whispered just enough for him to hear, "You know this isn't right."

"It doesn't matter. When in the presence of the Most Holy of the Maker it is as he commands with no question. You are faith-bound and are not allowed to speak unless in dictate states otherwise. Hand over your weapons and armor. Prepare yourself for sentence and penance," the second-in-command ordered.

The exactor obeyed. Immediately purists tied him to a nearby post from one of the burnt down buildings. Ser Metteros approached the bishop and bowed. He asked his eminence, "Your Most Holy, in the interest of expediting your exit out of this city in the name of Maker, may we forego the standard forty lashes all at once and divide them over time?"

"So be it," the man of power replied and stood regally in front of the rest of the contingent.

Metteros was handed a whip and approached the accused. "Ten lashes to begin your penance. You will receive the rest on our way back to the Citadel. Are you prepared?"

"Just get it over with," Tyberius replied harshly.

He waited for the pain to begin. First hit, then the second, each time the whip snapped there was extreme heat across the back. He hoped for some form of consolation in between the lashes. There was none because there was no time to recuperate, the whip continued to hit and bite across his neck, his back, and his ribs. His muscles would tighten in anticipation of the next blow but that just made it worse. They were on the seventh or eighth hit, he lost track, when he noticed a mob of rebels running into the street from down the road.

Behind him, he dimly heard the startled surprise from the purists about another group approaching from behind them. The Buckner guard and the insurgents of the rebellion collided in an all out brawl, fist to fist and club against bone. The purist warriors found themselves in the middle, unprepared for the onslaught of men that seemed possessed by the Defiler himself.

Tyberius, already defeated and weakened by the lashings, had no chance to fight back. The mob engaged, and tied to the post as he was, he could not move away. Bodies collided into him with bone-jarring force. The force of the impact made his head hit the post square-on and everything went black.

CONFESSION

How they made it to the most western stable building, and what was left of the contingent, was a miracle of the Maker. His Eminence was even proud how they had escaped the slaughter of the streets. It was not, however, without its price. There were only eight of them now with the bishop.

They were all huddled within the walls of the small stable structure with a few Buckner guards and two families of four. The three guards were waiting for a signal from outside. The rampage of the inhabitants of Westgate continued a few streets away. Through the windows and openings outside the building, more smoke was filling the streets from the chaos. The silence was broken by a loud coughing in one of the stalls. There were six horses in stalls not occupied with people.

Tyberius was on the dirt floor next to one of stalls that held a horse. He was tying a piece of fabric to his upper left leg to add pressure to the wound he received during their escape from the mob in the street. He was told that if not for Metteros cutting him down off the post and carrying him away, he would have been dead. During the sprint one of the insurgents tried to spear Tyberius, but only nicked him. Metteros managed to deflect the attack and one of the other warriors killed the assailant.

He winced as he tightened the fabric knot on the wound. His frame was ravaged from the whippings and battle, but the cut on the leg was not lethal, just a bleeder. He was thinking to himself on how it would have been nice to have a few female healers available.

His thoughts were interrupted by a purist who was no more than twenty-winters-old. "Exactor Tyberius, Ser Metteros requests your presence."

He slowly got up and followed the young man. As they approached one of the stalls, more coughing erupted from its area. When he turned the corner into it, there was Ser Carlum Metteros covered in blood. The bishop was hovering over him off to the right. He looked at Tyberius and shook his head. "He has asked for last rights, but wanted to talk to you before passing to the Maker."

The exactor nodded and bowed before the bishop. "I understand, Your Eminence," he replied. He knelt down next to the purist on his comrade's right side. The remaining contingent gathered all around them in a semi-circle with the bishop at the center near their fallen's head. "I am here, Metteros," Tyberius said.

The warrior opened his eyes and looked at the exactor. With his right hand he began reaching toward his left, and grabbed his mace. Tyberius noticed the extent of the damage done to the man. The left side of his head was indented. The chest cavity of his armor was opened wide by a spear or javelin that had been hastily removed. The coughing was from the blood filling his lungs and overflowing onto the ground around him. Metteros placed the mace on the center of his chest and had another coughing fit. Tyberius grabbed the man's hand on the mace. "Easy sir, just try small breaths, it will help." The damaged warrior nodded. Once he calmed down he hoarsely spoke, "You have to lead them."

"It's not my place or station," the exactor answered.

The fallen warrior looked at each one of the purists that were left around him and back to the exactor. "The next in command does not have your experience. You have to teach him."

The bishop then interjected, "You can't be serious. An exactor in command of a purist contingent? Blasphemous! He is a criminal of the Seat!"

Ser Metteros then looked hard at Ser Marodin Tarnis. "He is the best chance you have, my eminence."

"You have to get the bishop out of Buckner and back to the Citadel. You have to finish the mission," the warrior said as he turned back to face Tyberius.

The rogue looked down. "I'm not worthy of the Maker's warriors, Ser Metteros, as the bishop said."

The warrior priest coughed again, more blood came up, and now was exiting his mouth. He quickly composed himself and wiped the residue. "I was there. I know of your trial five winters ago, the theft of the Pontiff's rod of the Maker. You have been trying to make amends for that crime. I see the sadness in your eyes every time you are reminded."

He coughed again. "I don't have much time. Tarnis may not see what I see right now, because of our situation, but my faith in the Maker has shown me truth. I forgive you for your transgressions. You have been a blessing for my unit, and you do not have anything to prove to me or these men, not now or ever."

He wrenched in pain. "If I were not a religious warrior I too would have followed her into the depths of the Defiler's lair if I had been in your situation." He writhed in pain, crying out to the Maker.

Exactor Tyberius grabbed his hand around the mace and squeezed. "Ser Metteros, it's ok. She was a unique woman. Something I never met before in my life. I was young and defiant. You and your purist contingent only remind me of something I have forgotten, that's all."

Ser Carlum Metteros then let go of his hand and mace and reached up to the leather-armored man and with his bloodied open hand tapped the center of his chest plate. "Forgive me, Tyberius."

"For what, sir?" the exactor questioned.

His arm dropped back to his mace. "For the whipping…" he began another coughing fit.

The exactor smiled, "I forgive you, sir."

The dying man then announced, "My death request is this to all of you. Get his eminence to safety. Follow Exactor Tyberius' orders as if I were giving it. Tarnis, your Grace, I beg you. If I can forgive Tyberius for his sins, so can you with our Maker's blessing." He coughed again and more blood came forth.

He shuddered but forced his words out. He grabbed Tyberius' arm. "I know what is bothering you… Get the families out with you… I never got to start one… Get a message to my wife… Tell her I love her and will wait for her with the Maker." Then Ser Carlum Metteros exhaled his last breath.

As his arm dropped to the ground, the bishop came forth and placed his hands over the now dull, glassed eyes of the fallen warrior. "Be at peace, holy warrior. We will see you again." He turned to the rest of the warriors. "Make sure you bury him with honor. There is a small area next to a tree behind this building. Try to do it quietly and come get me when finished." The six other purists bowed and picked up their commander and exited. Tyberius began to go with them, when the Bishop called him. "Exactor, a word please."

He approached and bowed as his station commanded. "Yes, Your Eminence?" he asked

Bishop Tarnis turned to the exactor with a dark brooding look. "Out of respect for one of my most honorable purists, I will allow you to command until you train Ser Landry. Do you understand?"

"Yes, Most Holy," Tyberius answered.

"As for the families, they are not important. Your first mission is to me first and foremost," he commanded

"But you're...," he was interrupted.

The bishop came up to him, close to his face. "I will not be lectured by a criminal who has no connection to the church. The sinners of Buckner must pay the Maker's penance. We have lost many purists because of these abominations."

Tyberius then looked hard at the bishop. The look made the man back up. Tyberius wanted to attack him, and his eminence had no purist within sight.

"I am an exactor, Your Grace, one who works outside your inner workings. I am the one that does all the dirty work of the church. It is done so YOU can sit on your almighty altar and preach. I can be your greatest ally or your greatest threat! Out of respect to a Maker-loving man, I WILL honor his death request. I will get you to safety, first and foremost, but I WILL NOT sacrifice innocent people! I have been tried, convicted and under servitude to the enclave for five winters. I will do as I am commanded, but know this: my commander forgave me and I forgave him. Something the Maker has taught me: forgiveness.

"You keep pushing me and your chances of getting out of here drop drastically. I don't know if you have noticed, but a civil war has begun. We started with fifty but are now down to seven, including myself. I am finished with you condemning me. I submit to you now, have one of your purists break my contract with my death now. I'd rather join Metteros then put up with your constant reminding of how I followed a beautiful woman from my village of Bremingham and embarrassed you and your faith!"

The bishop shook his finger at Tyberius. "You...you...how dare you..."

He was then interrupted. "Your Most Holy...," a voice called.

The bishop and exactor turned to see a purist entering the opening of the stall they were in.

The religious man composed himself quickly. "Yes, Ser Landry?"

"We are ready, my Grace." the purist answered.

He moved past Tyberius and whispered, "Fine, exactor, but you will be responsible for the extra baggage. If you, or they, slow us down in any way, when we make it back to the Citadel you will find some additions added to your penance. Just with this insubordination I think you're back up to twenty!"

The exactor whispered back intently, "Why don't we just make it eighty and you administer it when we get back, IF we get there!"

The bishop looked at the hate-filled eyes of his exactor and realized it was best to take care of the honored dead before anything else happened. He then left with Purist Landry.

Once he left, one of the Buckner guards approached. "Excuse me, sir?"

"Yes," Tyberius answered.

"Our scouts have returned, and it is clear for now. They have two carriages that we can hook the horses up to and get your ambassador out of Westgate," he reported.

REPENTANCE

The first rays of the sun were out but not yet over the massive outer ring of the Sea of Walls. The wagons made their way out of Westgate, still within the shadow of the massive city of Buckner. Finally the road was before them. Off in the distance around some turns was the forest and safety. Each carriage that the Buckner guard acquired had a team of two horses. The maple and oak transports continued on the muddied cobblestoned path. The sounds of the horses' feet were comforting to Tyberius.

He was in the lead with the oak carriage, the two families of four inside. He was making sure that they would not slow down His Eminence. He had two purists with him as backup and lookouts. The other four were on the maple carriage, protecting the bishop. He and the other purists continued to scan the horizon in front and behind them for anything out of the ordinary. He did notice that at the top of the outer wall some sails were moving and coalescing into a group. Tyberius turned back to focus around the first bend that was easily a good mile and a half from the entrance of Westgate.

When they came into view of the slight ridge up ahead, he could see a gathering of individuals standing, blocking the way. They were all next to each other, the line extending north and south. He slowed the carriage to a stop and came down off the driver's seat. The other carriage stopped as he approached.

The bishop stuck his head out of the maple vehicle. "Why have we stopped?" The exactor pointed to all the people up on the ridge before them.

"I don't care. We need to get out of here. Run them over if you have to. This is not our fight," Tarnis replied.

They heard a low thump sound, then again, and again. It began with a few and started to pick up speed. Tyberius looked at the ridge. All the individuals were stomping their weapons, feet, or clanging their shields. A small roar started, they all began to scream a battle cry. It got louder and very deafening.

"They're going to attack Westgate," one of the purists called out.

Another added, "They don't stand a chance, and neither do we!"

Tyberius pointed and yelled to each of the purists. "All of you listen to me. Your first duty is to protect the bishop as Ser Metteros did!" He then pointed at the horde up on the ridge. "They may or may not attack, but if they do, by the Maker we will give them a fight they will not soon forget."

A loud horn went off over the sound of the yelling force. They began their decent slowly down the ridge then picked up speed toward the small caravan and Westgate. The ferocity in their eyes was frightening, as if the Defiler himself was in possession of the entire force.

The wall of bodies descended onto the two carriages, not giving a care if anyone was on, or in, them or not. At least a dozen of the rebels grabbed hold of the oak wagon and began rocking it to force it on its side. Tyberius could hear the screams of the families inside as it tipped over.

Another grouping rushed the purists and the exactor. Two humans were in mid-swing with their swords coming down onto Ser Landry. He was only going to be able to block one, but not the other. As he did, he closed his eyes, waiting for the blow that never came. He heard a thud and opened his eyes only to see Tyberius sending his rapier into a third adversary's eye socket. Landry's other target was on the ground with a throwing knife in his chest.

The exactor then leapt with the thin sword over a fourth. He spring boarded over the target's head and somersaulted with a twist. When he landed on his feet, he turned and stabbed the rebel in the back of the head at the base of the neck. Tyberius nodded in the purist's direction as to indicate "Go!" so that the young battle priest could gain the advantage.

Tyberius then, using his left hand, began grabbing and throwing immediately one…two…three…and finally four knives. Two more rebels fell. He glanced back to the purists protecting the bishop. Two more were carried away by the lynch mob. Their blood stained the ground as the mob slashed into them. Landry was at the door of the carriage, fending off three adversaries. Then the sunlight crested the Sea of Walls, blinding everyone.

There was the sound of something like thunder in the distance. A few moments' later explosions were all around the ridge. Screams, dirt, weapons, and body parts were flying everywhere. The bishop's vehicle was knocked over and rolled upside down from the concussive blast. Tyberius' face was scraped from sliding his head down on the stone road.

More thunder sounded. The exactor immediately rolled on his back to see the incoming cannon balls. He had mere seconds to react to the threat. Kicking his aching legs, with the injured one now bleeding again, he forced himself back into an upright position. As the cannon ball barrage came down, he was able to run just out of the blasts. More screams followed as parts of the two carriages splintered into many pieces. Shrapnel imbedded itself into his back, cutting through his leather armor. He ended up on his right knee but steadied himself with his left arm using his rapier. It bent under his weight.

He reached back and touched the piece protruding about a good six inches. Looking all around he could see more explosions along the line of the ridge and the fields between the trees and Westgate. The rebels were being slaughtered. "The ships that gathered on the outer ring...," Tyberius whispered. He realized what they were there for. Buckner was not going to stand for the insurgents infiltrating their great city. He checked his hand and saw the blood on it. He could feel the liquid going past the large splinter down the bottom part of his back, toward his right leg. *Not much time*, he thought.

"Help...me...please," he heard a voice off behind him.

He turned back toward the sound and saw the upside down, half-intact carriage the bishop was supposed to be in. More thunder roared and the rogue exactor ran toward the damaged vehicle, dodging and weaving even with the extensive pain. He ran, covering his face with the weapon hand, and slid as more dirt and stone and debris peppered him.

As he regained his bearings he found the bishop trapped under the carriage, with the weight of it on his chest. "I'm here, Your Eminence!" he called over the explosions.

The holy man reached with his hand, "Please, exactor... save me....by the Maker have mercy on me!"

Tyberius looked all around. There was nothing left of the contingent; all were dead. He quickly moved from the ground and positioned himself over what was left of the carriage. As he grabbed the large beam from the seat frame, he ordered the bishop, "When I lift, move, Your Grace!"

The man under him nodded. When the exactor lifted, the pain and force caused him to see stars. He felt the man move, and as he dropped next to him, he could hear him say, "Bless you, my child." More explosions all around them erupted and they covered each other from the debris.

"You're gravely injured, Tyberius. Can we make it to the tree line at least?" Tarnis asked.

The exactor, feeling weak, looked at their situation. The ships' fire was moving more and more toward the tree line to flush the rebels from their protective covering. He noticed a group running from Westgate. More rebels. The Buckner elite guard was pushing them out of their outskirt town and from the Sea of Walls. "We have to go back to Buckner, Your Eminence," Tyberius answered.

More explosions erupted again, more screams as what remained of the rebels ran past them. Ser Marodin Tarnis turned to the exactor. "You can't be serious. Go Back? We have to get out of here!"

Tyberius was about to answer when he heard a small child crying. He looked toward where the sound was coming from, the other carriage that had the families. He didn't pay attention to the bishop at that point, as the small figure appeared from the devastation all around.

The small boy couldn't have been more than three winters old. He was covered from head to toe in crimson red, all matted and dried. The only white was on his cheeks, from the tears. As more explosions came, the boy let out blood-curdling screams and covered his ears. He tried to run away from the blast but would fall down. He then tried to get back up, still crying, just wanting to get away from the madness all around him, wanting his mother and father calling out, "Mama...Dada!"

As weak as he was from blood loss, Tyberius gathered what strength he had left. He stood up, but the bishop grabbed him. "We have to get out of Buckner!"

"No...," Tyberius whispered.

"What?" Ser Marodin Tarnis questioned.

The exactor grabbed the bishop and stood him up. He looked into the scared man's eyes. The holy man could see the peace within him. Tyberius then told him, "All my life I have been running away from the man I was to become. No more. I left Bremingham in defiance of my father. I didn't want to be a farmer, I wanted more, and I was selfish. When that woman and her crew visited the inn I was fascinated by their travels, and her beauty. I ran away never thinking once how it impacted my family. How my father would feel losing a son. Now I see a boy, a child with no father, no mother, nothing. No way for him to say I'm sorry. No way to repay the woman that gave him birth. One thing your faith in the Maker has taught me is that nothing is to be taken for granted. We are to take care of who we can in this world. If we don't, who will? We have to protect the innocent. The Maker would, can we do no less? Go, Your Grace, run back to Buckner, the guards will protect you. I will be right behind you." With that, Tyberius ran toward the crying child.

The holy man looked at the exactor of his failed contingent, dodging and weaving the explosions, and for any that would try to stop him. He turned and began running back to Buckner.

Tyberius saw another set of explosions heading in the child's direction. He quickly changed direction to intercept the boy. The child was still crying loudly and looking frantically around. He bent down and scooped him up into his arms, still holding his rapier. He moved just in time as another explosion rang in his ears along with the child's screams. The pain throughout his body cried out. As he again changed direction to run back toward the bishop, a few rebels tried to take advantage. He quickly cut them down as he ran by. He ran as fast as he could toward the holy man to close the gap and to get to Buckner.

He couldn't have been more than twenty-five feet behind the Maker's Chosen when another series of cannon balls hit the ground. Even though he felt the pain and was aware that he lost his sword somewhere in the force of the blast, he held on tightly to the child. He did his best to cradle the boy and take most of the impact when he hit the ground.

The screams of the child snapped him back into reality. But he couldn't move. He felt weak. He still had the boy. The young child was trying to get away from the madness. Next thing Tyberius saw was the bishop. His robes were ripped in half, his face scarred on the right side from shrapnel. Ser Marodin Tarnis grabbed the child and the boy clung onto him and squeezed onto his neck, the bishop grimaced from the pain. He looked at the fallen exactor. "I'm sorry, my son. Your legs are gone."

Tyberius looked up towards Westgate. Buckner soldiers were approaching. They had routed the rebels from the war-torn town. He then smiled at the bishop. "It's ok, My Grace. It's my time, I have done what the Maker and Ser Metteros have asked: I've kept you alive. I only have one request."

The bishop, still holding the boy answered, "Yes, my son?"

Tyberius reached into a small compartment in his chest plate of the armor and produced a letter. "Can you get this to my family in Bremingham? Tell them how sorry I am and ask that they forgive me?"

The Bishop looked at the exactor with sadness and atonement. "Consider it done, Exactor Tyberius. May you pass unheeded to the Maker. All of your sins are forgiven. Say hello to Metteros for me."

The Buckner guard came up and Tyberius again smiled. They asked if the bishop was alright. The holy man let them know he would be ok. When he looked down, back to Tyberius, the man was gone.

The Buckner guard escorted the only two survivors of the first open field attack that would later become known as; the Westgate Massacre.

FAITH

Thirteen winters later…

The older religious man walked up stairs of marble and ivory. His bones ached from the exercise they were getting. His ornate satin white and red robe with gold trim flowed easily just above his feet. No more need for acolytes to hold the more form-fitting garment; he was using an ivory staff with a carved image of Jasia atop to counterbalance his weight. His pointed red velvet hat with gold trim let everyone know within the building he was the Bishop Missionary to the Jasian Enclave's orphanage of Buckner within the Sea of Walls.

He reached the top of the stairs and began his journey down the hallway toward the main auditorium. He passed many various pieces of art and sculptures. In the distance he could hear some speaking as he came closer to the entrance of the large space.

"…and as you all go forth from this place, you now have the skills and knowledge to be integrated back into society. Just know that The Maker will guide and protect you all of your days. Remember to take what you have learned here and be better men and women," the voice was saying. The old man recognized it as Ser Dextrose Rankin, one of the many teachers and priest leaders within the orphanage.

When he reached the threshold of the doorway, Ser Rankin saw him. The priest then called out to the audience, "All rise for His Eminence Ser Marodin Tarnis, original ambassador and founder of this very orphanage for the Maker in Buckner.

The young men and women did as they were commanded. Ser Tarnis approached the priest. "Would you mind if said a few words, Ser Rankin?"

"Not at all, Your Grace. It would be an honor," the priest replied.

Tarnis turned to the group and approached the edge of the small stage. The six foot tall man adjusted his stance with the confidence of his faith. His now black and grey hair protruded from the sides of his tall religious hat. Piercing blue eyes scanned the room, looking at each one of the orphans. He placed his hand behind him and began pacing back and forth, speaking. "You are the first, remember that. You have the potential to become what you were meant to be in the name of the Maker. We have taken you in when there was no one who cared."

He then stopped and faced the group again. "I wanted you all to know why I have come. I am here because I owe a debt to my Maker, my contingent, and an exactor who made all of this possible."

He reached into the folds of his robes and produced a letter. "For you see, my young men and women, I too was not immune to the wiles of the Defiler and his ways. I was lost in my own sin of pride and self righteousness. It took the loss of my entire contingent when this wretched civil war began to realize my folly."

He started unfolding the letter. "But out of that death and destruction, life was found as well. A life renewed by the Maker and his will and purpose. It allowed a small child to have a second chance when he lost everything.

An exactor, Tyberius, showed me this act of kindness when I was too lost in the chaos. He had only one request. To let his family know of his deeds. I did so as soon as I could."

He brought the letter up to read. "I now read to you the response I received from his family twelve winters ago. When I am finished I will ask you all a single question."

He took a deep breath and began reading the letter. "Your Eminence Tarnis, it is with great sorrow of his death we write back to you about our son Tyberius. We never understood why he left Bremingham until his and your letters. We did however have suspicions it had something to do with the traveling adventurers that came that spring before the planting season. His father and Tyberius had heated words about carrying on the family tradition. It was also with great sorrow to hear that he had become a criminal to the Jasian Enclave. However, we are glad that he had good people who looked out for him. We did teach him to accept the consequences of his actions as a young boy. We hope that this gives you comfort in knowing that even if you were hard on him, at times he would reflect on it, and become a better man. Even as our family is saddened by this turn of events, we, and his siblings, will carry on. We take comfort that you were with him in the end to send him to the Maker and he did not die alone. We are glad that he was able to at least save the child you mentioned. It gives us satisfaction that your purists did not give up on him and he was able, in return, to pass along that kindness, even if it meant his own life. May the Maker bless you and your enclave for saving our son's very soul. Signed, the Harkens."

He folded the letter back up and placed it back in his robes. "As you can see we are all able to do the Maker's will. It is our choice to do it or not. As we send you back into society, remember you have been given a second chance largely because of the sacrifice of Tyberius Harken. Use it wisely."

He then began to turn to walk away, when Priest Rankin stopped him. "Your Eminence, you were going to ask them a question."

"Yes...yes." He turned back to the group. "My question to you all is this: Would any of you consider following the faith and becoming a purist or priest in the name of the Jasian Enclave and the Maker?"

A young acolyte stood up immediately among the seats. The others looked at him for a moment.

The bishop called out, "What do you prefer, son?"

The young man yelled back, "I would like to become an exactor for the purists, Your Grace."

Ser Tarnis stared at him curiously. "What is your name, young man?"

"I am called Tyberius Carlum, Your Grace," the young man replied.

Then other acolytes within the audience began to stand up to volunteer for the Jasian Enclave as well.

4854 E.o.E

ONE WINTER PRIOR TO THE EVENTS OF STORMWIND

By:
Jay Erickson

A GOOD LIFE

Cyzer removed the heavy barding from his back. He felt the kink tense up in his left shoulder from the old dagger wound that he had received six winters prior. The wound had been deep, running down his shoulder, and across his back. He had missed living the life of a paraplegic by a hair's breadth. It sent a shiver down his spine, and a memory coursing through his mind of a different time, of Nix.

"Yer a lucky one, Cyz," a fellow soldier called from behind him.

Cyzer turned around and nodded to his brother-at-arms. "That I am, Kiefer," he replied.

Kiefer, a blonde headed, blue-eyed man in his early thirty winters smiled at Cyzer as he took off his armor as well. "Not many people can walk away from a wound like that," his partner remarked, as he always remarked, when they were disrobing together in the barracks.

Cyzer quietly dressed himself back into his fine tunic and trousers, strapped on his leather moccasins, and quickly exited the barracks. He tried to shake his mind of Nix, but the thought of him lingered. An odd feeling after so long.

He quickly signed out in the ledger, gathered his personal effects from the weapons locker, and proceeded home. It was just another day in the life of an exactor for the Jasian Enclave.

Some would call him a mercenary, as he owed no true affiliation to the religious nation state of Gurgen, but he preferred to think of himself as more of a freelance investigator. The Enclave sent him to solve the crimes that their pious soldiers couldn't sully their hands with. He dealt with the darker aspects of humanity, with foul magics, and seedy people. It was easy for him, given his past... in Rhacotis.

Again, he thought of Nix and sighed. Apparently, the man wouldn't be leaving his mind anytime today.

It didn't take him long to get home, a quick carriage ride out to the outskirts of Sentinel's Barrow, a distant piece of land where he built a nice manor for himself. Little came out this way, and that was what made it so great.

When he arrived he parked his carriage and took his steed to the stable. From there he made his way inside the manor. His servant, Jendris, stood ready to remove his overcoat and when done, handed him a small chilled snifter of brandy. He sat in his usual chair, in the study, and took a sip. He exhaled deeply as the cold liquid brought a soft burn to his chest, and he waited. Within moments, his daughter burst into the chamber.

"Dada, dada!" the little gold-haired child bellowed joyfully as she tore across the oaken boards and lunged into his legs, snaring them with a tight hug. He placed his glass down and picked her up, placing her in his lap.

His two-winter-old girl was a spitting image of her mother: vibrant golden tresses and big green eyes, so different from himself, with his darker complexion, brown eyes, and black hair. *A good thing*, he often told himself*, to see so little of the man he was, in his daughter before him.*

"Hello, love," his wife said from the doorway.

When Cyzer looked up, as he always did, he saw the silhouette of an angel. She smiled at him, her eyes radiating the love she felt for him. It was a good life. He knew that, and she was the reason for it. She had saved him.

THE PAST BECKONS

Cyzer awoke in the night to the rhythmic sound of ringing. It was a consistent sound, rising and falling in an odd, almost alien fashion. Like someone running a finger around the lip of a glass of water that was barely full.

It took him a moment to register what he was hearing, but when he did, his eyes popped wide open. *No!*

He moved his wife's arm from his chest. Her nude form rolled towards him, seeking his warmth. Slowly he placed a pillow between them and she grasped it eagerly. The sound of the ringing never once ceased.

He rose from the bed, placed his trousers back on, and walked bare-chested to his study. As he got closer the ringing intensified, as did the feeling in the pit of his stomach. It had been six winters…

Once in his study the sound seemed almost deafening to him, though in reality he knew it was barely distinguishable at all. It had been a private calling, a magical creation made for only the two of them when circumstances were most dire…

He reached out and pulled the book from the shelf. It vibrated softly in his hands. Carefully he opened it, revealing the false interior within and an amethyst crystal no larger than his thumb nestled against the packed pages. With trembling fingers he reached out and stroked the crystal. *This couldn't be just chance, not after today*, he said to himself.

Cyzer pulled the crystal free and walked over to the empty brandy snifter he had left on the table. He placed the crystal inside the glass.

"Cyzer," an all too familiar voice said deeply from the hollow vessel on the table.

"Nix," Cyzer returned, his voice nearly trembling as bad as his hands. "How did you get out?"

There was a long silence before the man on the other end answered. "The compound was getting too crowded. They released me on good behavior. I've changed, Cyzer."

Cyzer breathed a little easier. "That's good to hear."

"Listen," the voice said. "We need to meet. Can we meet?"

Cyzer bit his lower lip in thought. He had ended this past for a reason; he had a new life now, a better life. "I don't know..."

"I need your help, Cyzer. I'm not the man I was, not anymore. Please, meet with me."

Cyzer grit his teeth and punched his favorite chair. Nix at one time had been his best friend. If he was sincere, if he was real in his desire, how could Cyzer tell him no? What if the roles were reversed? "Sure, Nix. Where do you want to meet?"

"I'm in the area," Nix told him. "I could... I could come by."

Cyzer shook his head. "Cassandra doesn't want to see you, Nix. She would be furious that we are even talking."

"Outside then? Can we meet outside? By your compost heap, so she won't see us," Cyzer noted that his voice was almost pleading. He really does need my help...

"Okay, we'll meet out back," Cyzer agreed.

He ran his fingers through his hair as he heard a sigh of relief from the crystal. "Thank you." Then the crystal fell flat, its subtle vibrations gone.

Cyzer closed his eyes and took a deep breath. *Nix,* he thought. After six winters, it was really him. His best friend, his partner, and the man he had betrayed for a woman...

THE MEET

Cyzer's chest grew tight as he walked out to the edge of his property line. He and Nix had gotten this plot of land together, back when they had worked their criminal circles in Rhacotis. They had always planned to expand their smuggling ring here into Gurgen, into the heart of the Jasian Enclave where it would be the most lucrative, and the most dangerous.

After their last bust though, when Nix got pinched, Cyzer did away with that life. He had taken his wealth, and Cassandra, and started a clean living on the land that was once going to do ill. He used his knowledge of criminal circles and smuggling to land him his job as an exactor, and he was good at it. Really good.

Therefore, it was no surprise that Nix knew exactly where he was now. Cyzer had never thought Nix would see the light of day again. The sorcerers of Rhacotis were not very forgiving, especially when it was their property that was being smuggled.

As he approached the heap he could see a simple carriage waiting on the other side. It was a single horse drawn carriage, same engraving, and same design as his own. Nix was leaning against the front wooden spoked wheel. He was holding a folded piece of cloth in his hands.

Nix looked haggard and gaunt. He had lost so much weight, Cyzer realized. His brown hair had thinned considerably and he had just enough growth on his face to be considered a beard. It was lined with gray. His hazel eyes regarded Cyzer, hopeful.

"Hey Cyz," he said passively. "You look good."

"Thanks," Cyzer replied apprehensively.

Nix held up the cloth. It was a tan face wrap adorned in silver piping, a common fashion in Rhacotis for women of higher station. "I found this... in our old place. I think it was Cassandra's. I was hoping..." he shrugged. "Peace offering or something."

Cyzer crossed his arms. "It's not hers."

"Oh," Nix said dejectedly. Cyzer watched as he threw it into the compost heap. "There were so many women back then, weren't there?" he added with a chuckle. "Opium and wine, too. After chasing the dragon so long, I guess it's hard to keep track. It's all is so blurry now."

Cyzer didn't need this. "I didn't come here to reminisce, Nix. What did you need?"

Nix stood up straight. "Sorry, you're right. I came because… Cyz, I'm in trouble man. I had nowhere else to go."

Cyzer felt the anxiety in his gut turn to dread. He felt his arms drop. "What did you do?"

"I wanna be free, man. I want a good life, a life like you made. I want to do things differently. I don't want to go back ever," Nix began.

"What did you do?" Cyzer asked again.

Nix began to pace near the wheel, shaking his head. "When I got out I used the rest of my wealth to get this carriage, started my own legit business, ferrying people. Honest people. I've been doing all right. I mean, man we know the roads and trails so well. And it's felt so good, doing it real."

"What did you do, Nix?" Cyzer said with an edge to his voice.

Nix sighed and shook his head and when he spoke his voice trembled with fear. "It's not my fault, Cyz. I swear." He stepped to the side of the wheel and Cyzer could see long ruts against the wheel. Many spokes were splintered and cracked, and the housing warped. It was covered in blood.

Cyzer came forward immediately. Inside the carriage, he could see the still form of a young woman.

Nix was crying. "It was dark. She came out of nowhere, right into the wheel. I was moving at a good pace. It all happened so fast. I don't understand. She had to have seen me. What was she thinking?"

Cyzer was numb. He didn't know what to say, what to think. "You… you brought her *here*?" he stammered.

Nix looked at Cyzer, his eyes full of terror. "What was I gonna do? I'm a former criminal, already imprisoned once in the worst compound on the continent. I wouldn't get a trial, or anything fair and you know it, Cyz. Next step for me is a hanging."

Cyzer grabbed the bridge of his nose and squinted his eyes in thought. He knew Nix was right. There would be no fair trial for him, accident or not. He was a public menace now. They would kill him and be done with it.

"What do you expect me to do?" Cyzer asked bluntly.

Nix shook his head. "I don't know... you're... you're an exactor now, right? A law-keeper of sorts. You know how to make this stuff disappear, right?"

Cyzer stared at Nix incredulously. "Disappear!" he roared.

"Shhh!" Nix said looking around as if they were still in a populated area, instead of the western hills of Sentinel's Barrow.

Cyzer pointed at the prone body in the carriage. "There is a dead woman on my land, and you are asking me to make it disappear!"

"They're going to kill me!" Nix pleaded. "Even though I've changed, they won't care."

Cyzer sighed and paced as well. "No, they won't," he agreed.

"I'm different now, I swear it," Nix begged. "Please help me."

Cyzer looked at the body, and then at his friend. In the past, they had given up everything for each other. Cyzer had even taken a knife in the back for the man. Nix had meant that much to him once. His left shoulder tightened as if in response to his thoughts.

The sincerity in Nix's eyes was indisputable. *This was an accident*, Cyzer told himself. It could happen to anyone. Nix just had bad luck. Did he deserve to die for it?

"Fine. I'll help. Let's get shovels."

THE ACT

They walked out deep into the hills, far away from any of the bustle of Sentinel's Barrow or anywhere near the well-worn road.

Nix, now a nervous wreck, was in no condition to try to carry the body. So Cyzer had her slung over his shoulder as he made the long walk.

Blood seeped down from her torn face and ran in long rivulets across his back. His tunic was ruined. From what he could tell, she looked at one time to have been a very beautiful young woman. Dark hair and dark eyes. A similar complexion to both he and Nix. It was such a shame.

When they reached beyond his property and into the neighboring lands, he stopped.

Nix looked around. "I remember when we looked at this place," he told Cyzer. "We said not here. Too many hills."

Cyzer, breathing heavily, nodded. "Reminded us too much of our childhood."

Nix chuckled, "Agonthill Highlands. That was a lifetime ago. First Rhacotis, then the Highlands, then back to Rhacotis, now here. We've really moved around."

Cyzer looked at his friend. "That we have."

"So we choose the neighboring plot instead!" he added with a laugh. Strangely enough, Cyzer found himself chuckling too.

"Guess it doesn't make much sense, does it?" he agreed.

"Young and dumb," Nix said.

Cyzer could definitely agree with that.

Cyzer placed the body on the ground, and together they began digging. Sweat lacquered his body as they dug deeper and it made Cyzer start thinking. Perhaps when this was over, he and Nix could really have a fresh start. They had been friends since they were small children. They had done everything together. It had taken a woman for Cyzer to see the error of his ways. Maybe that's what Nix really needed: a good woman.

Then Cyzer felt a pang of regret as he remembered Cassandra had been Nix's woman first.

"Nix... I... I want to say I'm sorry... for the way everything turned out," Cyzer began.

There was a loud snap, and Nix cursed as his shovel snapped in half. He reached up and sucked on the wound it left on his hand, staring at Cyzer angrily.

"Things turned out pretty shitty, Cyz," he said with no trace of forgiveness in his voice.

"I... know," Cyzer said as he kept digging. "I've been thinking about it, over and over. I want to help. I want to make things right between us."

Cyzer noted Nix's eyes were cold as he looked back at him. "You want to help? *Now* you want to help? I was rotting in a sorcerer's prison for six long winters, placed there by the Arch-Magus Cardica himself. It doesn't get any more damning than that. Do you know what that does to you? What they do to you?" he said aggressively.

Cyzer looked at the ground in shame. Slowly he kept shoveling more dirt away. Nix continued, "I've lost things there I can never get back, and what did you get? A fresh life, good health, and my woman."

Cyzer reflexively stared at him, wide-eyed. "It wasn't like that!"

Nix grunted disgustedly. "Right. Then why didn't we both get pinched that day, Cyz? We both know Arch-Magus Cardica hated you after that tryst with one of his thirteen daughters. Left her impure, as I recall. No longer suitable for marriage."

Cyzer didn't answer... he couldn't answer. For nothing he could say would be anything different than the truth that was just laid out before him. He had betrayed his best friend, to the very man they were smuggling from, for his woman, pure and simple.

"I'll tell you what, Cyz. You want to help so bad all of the sudden?" he said as he picked the broken shovel out of the churned ground. "Dig the fucking hole yourself."

With that, Nix stormed off and left Cyzer with his thoughts. Dark thoughts of his murky past and all of his betrayals. And so Cyzer did what Nix wanted. He dug.

~ ~ ~

It was nearly dawn when the hole was deep enough. Cyzer, covered in grime and the blood of the dead woman, stripped down and threw his tunic into the hole along with the body. He then began to throw the dirt back on. It didn't take nearly as long as digging alone.

A short time later he watched as Nix came lumbering back, his head held low. "Look Cyz…," he began, "I'm sorry. I was out of line."

Cyzer sighed. "I deserved it," he said.

Nix shook his head. "No, you deserve more than I gave you. You… you're really doing something here for me. Though the last six winters may have been shit, this… this is going to keep me alive."

Cyzer nodded, but stayed silent.

After the act was completed, they walked back towards his property. The sun was beginning to crest over the hills when they made it back to the carriage.

"You have great taste in carriages at least, Nix," he said after their long silence.

Nix nodded and smiled. "I guess some things *don't* change."

Cyzer looked over to the strung-out man with regret. He had done this to him, made him this way. He only hoped this helped. "Nix…"

The frail man held up his hand, stalling the words. "Thanks for this," he told Cyzer. "Above all else, thanks as an old friend. I'll be in touch."

With that, he climbed into the carriage and rode it away. The damaged wheel crunched and ground, but it still held up under the weight. For how long, Cyzer couldn't say.

Slowly he made his way back to the rear entrance of his manor.

CHECK

Cyzer placed the shovel out back and managed to slip in quietly before anyone noticed. He quickly drew himself a bath and scrubbed the filth of the night before off him. When he emerged he was clean, but hardly refreshed. What he had done troubled him. Though it was an accident, he had hidden the manslaughter of a woman. He didn't even know who she was.

His daughter came into the room and wrapped herself around his legs. "Dada! Dada!" she squeaked gleefully.

She had been someone's daughter.

"Good morning, love," Cassandra said as she rounded the corner. "Did you have trouble sleeping last night? You were out all night."

She could have been someone's mother.

Cyzer shook his head as he walked to his study. From there, there was a large balcony from where he could see his whole property; namely, as far back as the compost heap. He stared out of the large glass windows at the heap where he had met Nix. Behind him, Jendris dropped off a fresh snifter of brandy.

"Shall I take the old one, sir?" the man asked.

Cyzer turned to look at him, vacantly, until he saw that his servant was holding the glass with the amethyst crystal in it. "That's okay; I'll take care of it."

The man nodded. "As you will, sir." As he turned to walk away, he turned once more to face Cyzer. "Did you take the carriage out last night, sir?"

"Excuse me?" Cyzer asked, perplexed.

"The carriage," Jendris replied. "I only ask because when I came in this morning it was moved, and it looks like it hit something. You didn't hit an animal yesterday, did you?"

Cyzer grew pale.

Then the ringing began.

Jendris looked down at the empty glass curiously. Cyzer rushed forward and took it from him. "Thank you, Jendris. That will be all."

Confused, Jendris merely nodded and walked out of the room.

Cyzer looked down at the glass in his hand. "Hello, friend," Nix said, his voice dripping with sarcasm.

"What have you done?" Cyzer demanded.

The glass laughed at him. "Only what you had coming to you."

"I'm an exactor," Cyzer threatened, "and I know what you did."

"What *I* did?" Nix said chuckling. "Walk to the window."

Cyzer turned back to the balcony window. As he did, he saw a Jasian carriage pull up to the compost heap.

"Three days ago, the Arch-Magus received a certain ransom letter for the life of one Sybia Cardica. You don't know her, being that she was a little young for your tastes six winters ago at around the age of twelve, but I'm sure you recognize the surname," the voice sneered as Cyzer watched his 'partner' Kiefer climb out of the carriage and make his way to the mound.

"Sybia was an emissary for the peoples of Rhacotis. As you know, the nation of Malten, where Rhacotis resides, and the nation of Gurgen, home to this sleepy town you live in, are not exactly on good terms. She was here to change that," Nix continued.

"Now, some good neighbor just happened to tip off the Jasian Enclave as to her whereabouts, and right about now they are going to find something of hers."

Cyzer could only stare, mortified, as the man lifted up the tan face wrap Nix had thrown there the night before.

"As exactors go, I hear they are pretty thorough. They are going to see that the spokes of your carriage were used to kill the poor woman and of course there is the matter of the shovel with freshly churned dirt on it at the back of your manor."

"I'll expose you," Cyzer hissed.

"I have an alibi," Nix replied. "Where were you last night? Did anyone notice you missing, by chance? Did you mention me to your wife? How are you going to explain where you've been? Or better yet, how are you going to explain your tunic covered in the victim's blood buried with her, out in a set of hillocks that looks strikingly like your childhood home? I'm sure you've told Cassandra why it is that you like this place so much."

"I wonder what the sentence is for something like raping and murdering an emissary of Rhacotis? Pretty sure a straight hanging is just too good for the likes of you. After all, you did have a thing for the Arch-Magus' daughters before," the voice said sinisterly.

Cyzer could only whisper, "How could you?"

"I told you from the beginning that I've changed, Cyzer. You never asked how, you only assumed that it was like you. I guess in a way it was, for I'm the betrayer now."

Cyzer was silent.

Nix, however, turned dark. "You owe me, Cyzer. You turned on me and took everything I held dear! Well I'm here to collect, and you are way **past due**."

The vibrations stopped. Cyzer heard a knock on the door and Jendris answer. There was yelling down the hallway followed quickly by heavy footfalls and the screaming of his wife. Somewhere in the distance, his daughter began crying.

Numb to it all, he reached down and replaced the crystal glass with the small chilled snifter of brandy. He sat in his usual chair, in the study, and took a sip. He exhaled deeply as the cold liquid brought a soft burn to his chest.

And he waited...

4855 E.o.E

ONE WEEK AFTER THE EVENTS OF STORMWIND

By:
J. P. Strohm

CHAPTER I

The sky around the Agontill Highland hillsides was still filled with the wisps of grey smoke. It was an ever-present reminder of the burning of Agot, and the horror of the attack from the 'Wilds'.

A walled structure stood firmly off in the distance, about a mile away. It was a monastery just to the northwest, and it seemed to be the only building to escape the assault on the town.

To her east, about one hundred yards away, there was a small outcropping of makeshift fencing. It was made of wood and stone and stood away from the town. Processions of a few people were making their way into it carrying a small pine box, with mourners following behind. It was obvious that it was the coffin of a small child. Another innocent caught in the slaughter of the attack.

The mourners, all dressed in black, with the women covering their faces in veils, were still hunched over as they moved forward. Some of the men were at the women's sides to hold them and steady their walk. Even then, she saw at least one stumble, and try to back up away from the cemetery due to the grief.

The young man attending her stopped with the woman, seemed to say something, and then helped her press forward with the others. Her cries could be heard on the wind like a melancholy lullaby of pain and suffering. It was like a bard's tale of an adventure that did not have a happy ending.

She stood there for a moment watching in silence before turning her gaze back to the southeast toward the Trade Road. That road led to Ethens and the Lugos Mountains. That road led away from all this pain.

She adjusted her platemail helmet, with center nose guard. While it obscured her features and covered most of her shoulder length brownish-red hair, her green gaze was not obstructed by the overcast shadow of the head covering. Just inside that protective shell she could feel her petite nose just barely touch the nose guard. They had sized it perfectly for her, of course. Her thin lips and narrow jaw line were the only things exposed through the opening, and that was the most anyone saw of her face.

The rest of her armor was as fitted as her helmet. It hugged her five-foot-eight-inch frame, but not so tightly that it limited her movements in battle. It was still dusty and had dents and scuffs. Visible signs of battle.

Overlaid upon the armor was a light blue tabard with a circumpunct symbol. That emblem was meant for one under the service of the Jasian Enclave.

Attached to her right hip was a throwing axe; on her left, a longsword. Protruding from her back on the right side was the wooden figure of a contorted face with black eyes and white, sharp teeth. Various tattoos trailed down the weapon's stock. It somewhat looked like a monster, and also like a bow facing down. It was ornately decorated and unique to her alone. The special crossbow had a chamber off to its left side, set at a forty-five degree angle. This monstrosity held five chambers of quarrels ready to dole out death.

She heard the crunching footsteps of someone approaching from behind. The woman turned around as the man called out, "Exactor Raven, a word please."

Raven sighed and slowly approached the younger man of his late twenties, early thirty winters. He was well built, and tall. A warrior who was clad in similar platemail armor, but he carried a large battle mace and a kite shield, all adorned in the classic Enclave symbols.

When she was about ten feet from him she stopped and placed her right arm across her chest. Raven bowed slightly from the shoulders and lowered her head and eyes to the ground. "Purist Amháin, how can I serve the Maker and the Enclave?"

He returned the greeting, and announced. "The Maker requires your particular divine skills that will allow you entrance into his presence and redemption of your transgressions... again."

"To which of these skills do you refer, Purist Amháin? Is it my blade, my axe, or my crossbow?" she asked as she stood up straighter.

"Maybe all, but first you must find what it is the Maker and the Enclave wishes you to locate."

"Tracking then", she replied.

Amháin turned back towards Agot. "Walk with me, Exactor." It came off as a request, yet Raven knew it was otherwise.

She nodded and began her walk next to the purist. She stayed to his right, only half a step behind. They began the trek down the small hill. Shortly after, another battle-clad purist ran past them up the slope to take her place as sentry to the town and the Trade Road.

Raven walked quietly next to the large man, waiting for him to speak. She was an exactor, and it wasn't her place to speak to a purist unless first spoken to.

She knew her role well. Exactors were specialists contracted by the Enclave to do their dirty work. This gave the church plausible deniability in case an exactor committed an atrocity that didn't exactly follow in line with the religious nation's way of thinking. Raven's contractual obligation was like many exactors. She was given a choice after her trial; death or indentured servitude. She was part of a group that stole something that was claimed could not be stolen while within the monolithic walls of the Citadel. It resided within the seat of the Gurgen Kingdom, The Supreme Pontiff's Rod of the Maker. A legendary symbol, and only touched by men of the god himself.

They had it for exactly three minutes.

Arrest, battery, and subsequent trial followed. During the trial, when asked why Raven did it she replied sarcastically, "I just wanted to be the only woman in the realm that could say I held the Maker's rod". She then added a gesture that suggested sucking on a smoking stick.

The uproar that followed amongst the purist judges alone was almost worth her execution. Never had such holy men used more colorful language. Her defense council pleaded to have her spared due to her unique skill set. She would serve The Maker and it was, after all, the duty of all purists to convert the unconvertible. So the choice was given to her and the group involved: serving the Enclave, or dying.

They were all divided to separate purists units shortly afterwards. She had been under contract now for the last seven winters, under Purist Aodhfin Bray's contingent, looking for a sorceress named Ambrosia. That led her to this moment, and this town-- Agot. A town that, when they arrived, they found in shambles from an attack by the Wildmen from the south.

Soon after, Aodhfin Bray left Amháin in charge of the contingent and set out with a monk from the Order of the Sacred Fist and a High Elf. Goldhym was their title, if she wasn't mistaken.

Amháin did not disclose the nature of Bray's mission, but informed all that they needed to continue to search Agot for the sorceress, or any evidence thereof.

That was a week ago.

Raven's thoughts were interrupted by Amháin. "It seems that another Master of the Order of the Sacred Fist is missing. There is some disorder amongst the order. We believe that the master was assisting in the defense of the town and may not be accounted for yet."

"How is that?" she asked as she looked toward the town and the monastery in the distance. She glanced back to the purist. Raven never lost step with him. "How can they not notice him gone for this long?"

"According to eye witnesses, Master Ferric was last seen on the west side of town taking on three Wildmen. When the enemy withdrew it was assumed he was still there attending to the injured. The monks said he was well known in that section and had acquaintances there. He may have stayed to make sure they were in satisfactory condition," Amháin answered. "The order can function with two masters, but now there is but one."

Raven noticed that as they approached the town's main entry road two other exactors and another purist were there. They seemed to be waiting for them.

She recognized the other purist immediately. It was Ceartas, Amháin's temporary second in command. He was a battle-tested warrior and skilled healer with Creative magic. The man was carrying a large silver mace and a small round shield. His armor glinted in the sunlight. Ceartas was well known for keeping his gear clean at all times. He once claimed, "The Maker allows me to blind his enemies with His brilliance to serve righteous justice to those who are not of the Maker's will, or in repentance of their sins."

It was no secret that he would spend hours cleaning and polishing the gear after every battle, only taking a break for sustenance or sleep. Some even said that when healed by him on the frontlines, "It was like the Maker himself was in attendance within the glow of light around him." Many found the experience so uplifting that right after the healing they would jump back into the fray of battle to prove themselves to the Maker and His will.

Raven could understand just by looking at the charismatic five-foot-eleven-inch man. His piercing blue eyes and brightly colored blonde hair also seemed to carry the Maker's presence in the man himself. She smiled slightly as she thought to herself, "*Being away so long from the Citadel, I wonder how devoted he truly is under that entire posh exterior?*"

Her thoughts were interrupted. "Exactor Raven, please control your impulses. Do not think the contingent has not known how you look upon Ceartas. I would not want to have you succumb to your earthly desires just to be marked with the stigma of a sinner. Nor do we wish to have the righteous be tempted by the Defiler's temptress. Your duties are to purge yourself and sanctify yourself before the Maker," Purist Amháin quietly remarked to her as they came within earshot of the group.

Raven immediately composed herself in a more professional manner. "Understood, Purist Amháin, please forgive my roguish thoughts. I am but a simpleton in the Maker's great plan of Kuldarr. Your council and wisdom are, as always, a benefit and merciful in keeping servants such as myself on the path to righteousness," she replied.

"You may need much righteousness from the Maker in order to find this Master of the Order," the purist responded.

She was about to ask why when one of the other exactors next to Ceartas approached. "Ah! Exactor Raven, good to see that you will be assisting us with this small expedition." She had only seen and heard of him within the contingent but never really met him before. He extended his right hand in greeting, a Fermanian greeting. He was from the East.

Raven took the five-foot-three-inch man's hand and shook it. "Trodaire Casein, right?" she responded. The muscular human in the platemail armor shook his head yes in acknowledgement. She saw that he had both a javelin and bastard sword strapped across his back, a curious combination.

The other exactor moved forward and Trodaire turned his head in acknowledgement. "Of course you already know Dwyn Lani, our man of multiple other talents."

Dwyn was not dressed in platemail as the others, but in studded leather. The armor was gaudily decked out in bright hues of blue and the symbols of the Jasian Enclave. He was short for a man, standing at mere five-foot-two-inches. He looked like he could weigh only about a hundred fifteen pounds soaking wet. And that was with his armor.

Dwyn Lani wasn't a battler. As such, he was only armed with a decorative rapier and quite a few throwing knives. He also sported a short bow on his back with a quiver of arrows. Raven envied him. She knew she could move far better with that type of armor but she had yet to prove her loyalty to the cause of the Maker, according to Amháin, anyhow.

She and Dwyn on occasion, when nobody was around, would sit and smoke some of the Spriggan's rare leaf and talk about their lives before their service to the Jasian Enclave. Both remembered what it was to be carefree and be on adventures to make a name for each other within the realm of Kuldarr. They both agreed that Amháin had it in for her, in particular, since day one of her induction to the contingent. Raven was the only female exactor within Bray's contingent; all the other women were healers. They had yet to figure out the reason for his animosity towards her. She nodded to Trodaire and acknowledged Dwyn. "Yes, we have consulted on many subjects of combat and survival skills we both have in common."

The trio of exactors was quickly interrupted by Amháin, "Good then. You will all have the basic resources you need to complete what is necessary by the Maker's will. Return the monk to the Order and restore order to the town of Agot. Additionally, eliminate any other threats left over from the previous attack."

Ceartas interjected, "I would suggest we begin right away and determine what has happened to Master Ferric by getting over to the west side of town."

Raven nodded to the others and toward Amháin. "Agreed we must find these acquaintances and see what they can tell us."

Amháin looked in the direction they needed to go. "May the Maker bless you and protect you on this journey, and find your purpose within his will." He deftly moved past them and headed back into town. About halfway around the corner of the building by which they were standing, he turned back toward Raven. "Remember, Exactor Raven, do not stray from the path or you will be forever the Defiler's bitch." He then disappeared around the corner.

Dwyn smiled at Raven after the purist left. "He really doesn't like you, does he?" he asked.

"Guess not," she answered with a shrug of her shoulders.

Ceartas looked between the two. "Well he has a lot on his mind since Bray left. I know that is no excuse, Exactor Raven, for the way he has treated you for the last seven winters."

She placed her hand on her hip. "Do you know why he has been that crass with me since I was assigned?"

"He has never liked the exactors. He believes that your caste will corrupt the Enclave in the long run. You being a woman in the contingent compounds the fears he has," Ceartas replied

Dwyn chuckled, "Guess a woman's place is in the healing tents, eh?" Dwyn skirted into the town quickly not waiting for a reply from Raven.

Trodaire gave a quick smirk at Raven and turned to Ceartas. "I am sure he was just joking. I don't think he meant any harm or disrespect toward the contingent's healing staff or to Exactor Raven."

The battle healer lifted his left arm and placed his hand on Trodaire's right shoulder. "Far be it from me to question the Maker's divine will on what and who he uses in the great scheme of things. Just because I have pledged my devotion to the Enclave doesn't mean I am no more a man than Dwyn." He let go of the shoulder then smiled toward the pair of exactors, "Besides, even I have been injured many times and have found the women healers' skills very spiritually uplifting. They have a rather tender touch, in the name of the Maker of course. Now let's get on with this investigation."

Raven smiled at Trodaire then began moving into the town. The exactor fighter just shook his head and began following after the group. "This is going to be one interesting investigation," he said as he jogged past Raven to catch up to the battle healer and Dwyn.

As she looked at the three walking before her entering the town square, she then added under her breath, "Yes, this is going to be very interesting indeed."

CHAPTER II

The town square of Agot was not as busy as it once was. The dry dirt paths in between the buildings and main area still had darkened spots from the previous attack, an unpleasant reminder where the blood of many had spilled. The daub and timber buildings were arranged in a square pattern around the town's large well. The area was approximately one hundred feet in any given direction from the well. Usually a few carts between the well and buildings would be scattered about, perhaps ten to twelve at any given time of the day. Now there were only four. The group didn't need to be reminded why.

As the investigators made their way over to the east side of the square, Raven's eyes settled on the burnt remains of a single child's moccasin. There was no other to match it; it stood alone. Images of the woman collapsing into tears at the funeral only scant hours before danced through Raven's green eyes.

She was barely aware that the half-collapsed building Ceartas led them to was once the bakery. Just outside a young man in his late teens was sweeping the front porch area. As Raven realized where she was, she saw that the right side of the building was folded in on itself, exposed to the elements. Inside she saw that it was the living quarters of the baker and his family.

The shop itself was still intact and boards were already in place to shore up and begin rebuilding the living area. A group of young men and an older gentleman were hammering new pieces of wood. Others placed the bad wood into the alley area between the bakery and building next door.

The young man sweeping took notice of the group and stopped his task. Placing the broom at the door frame, he stated, "I am afraid we are done for the morning until the afternoon. You have missed the morning rush, what there was of it." He then placed himself between them and the bakery.

Ceartas quickly replied, "That's fine young man, but we are here on a more investigative matter."

"Investigation?" he asked, looking back to the shop, confused. "Our damage was from the Wilders, not some vandals within our town."

Dwyn interjected, "We know. We are looking for someone that would visit your shop every once in a while."

The young man seemed to tense up, and his posture took a more surprised and shocked stance, as if he was to be questioned about some dark secret from long ago. He quickly bought both hands open- palmed in a non-confrontational manner. "Look, if this about Jaclyn, I can explain."

Raven rolled her eyes, while tilting her head to the right and sighing. She pushed through the group of investigators to stand in front of the young man. He was startled a bit and shifted like he wanted to run. Raven held up her hand to indicate he should stop. "Look, we are not concerned with your love life. We are looking for Master Ferric from the Order of the Sacred Fist. Our investigative team…" She moved her left hand to the left across the group now behind her. "… obviously has some information that indicates you may know him or who he visits on the west side of town."

"Ah you mean the guy in the white robe, dark-skinned, dark hair and eyes. Not from around these parts, maybe from Malten. Lives in the monastery?" the young man asked.

Trodaire chuckled behind Raven, and moved his left balled-up fist to cover it up like a cough. Dwyn then answered, "I think that would be him. You know… monastery… white robe… maybe some sandals… doesn't seem to carry any weapons…a Master of the Sacred fist. You do know that anyone that lives in a monastery is a monk, right?"

"Look we are busy every morning with lots of people and I don't pay attention to all that kind of stuff. We have orders to fill. All I know, he doesn't talk much. All I ever got out of him was he lives at the monastery and every two weeks he comes to pick up an order of breads, grains, and pies for one of the old town's founders, and he always overpays with three silver pieces," the young man replied, miffed at the group.

Ceartas moved up next to Raven's right to be closer to the young man. He smiled politely and gestured with open arms. "Look son, if you know the name of this founder it will help us locate Master Ferric faster. Then we can move along and let you get back to more important business."

The young man placed his hand under his chin while looking down at the ground, tying to recall anything the investigators wanted. "You said on the west side of town, right?" he asked.

"Yes," Raven replied

He looked up, taking his hand away from his chin and pointed at the group. "I think its founder Loach Hynafin, but I am not sure. You may need to speak with Norna Dewin, the grumpy old witch. She knows everything on that side of town."

"Did he say a witch?!" Trodaire exclaimed from behind Raven and Ceartas. As he began to move forward, Dwyn grabbed his right arm to halt him. Ceartas looked back toward the exactors and then back to the young man with a look of concern and determination. "I hope that she is not indeed a witch as you say, young man. Our contingent has been pursuing a sorceress in these parts for some time. If she is involved with Master Ferric's disappearance, things will turn very ugly very quickly for this woman. By the Maker's will she shall see justice and reconciliation for all her sins."

Raven placed her left arm across Ceartas's chest, also slowing his advance. Gracefully she removed her helmet and cradled it against her hip. "I don't think she's really a witch," she said to the trio of men. Raven turned her attention to the young man now, her eyes lit with fire. "I would suggest you explain your last statement, boy. I, being an exactor under the Jasian Enclave, am under obligation to eradicate all threats before they become a problem. The Enclave gives us wide range of discretion."

The boy could only stare at her in confusion.

Raven sighed. "Let me put it to you this way. If the Jasian Enclave had evidence to prove any evil existed here in Agot, your town would be purged. Substitute the exactors with the Wilders. All would be destroyed or taken to be sanctified at Gurgen. Do you understand?"

The young man turned pale white at the statement. His lower lip quivered as he tried to find the words. He took a deep breath, swallowed, and found his courage. "Norna is not a witch. All of us as children called her that. She is always crabby, and scolds everyone about not doing things the way she did them back in the day. She used to be an alchemist; word has it she still is. All she ever wants is to be left alone.

The rumor has always been that she was a witch. I do know that when anyone pulled a prank on her, the Mayor and council had a visit from Loach the very next day, and those responsible were caught and required to undo the wrong."

The rest of the investigative team came forward to the young man. Raven lowered her arm off Ceartas and just stared at the young man. Trodaire then spoke. "This Loach sounds like a man of action." He moved to Raven's right. Dwyn went to the battle healer's left.

"Then why is a Monk of the Sacred Fist getting him food supplies every two weeks? If he is capable of coming into town to correct a wrong to someone, why can't he pick up basic needs?" Dwyn inquired.

Ceartas looked to the troop. "I guess we should go ask this so- called witch," he said as he winked at Raven. He then brought his attention back to the young man. "We will get to the bottom of this, ser, by the Maker's will. I pray that what you have told us is true. If not, the Maker will have you reveal more to us if we return."

"It is, ser! I swear by the life of my mother and father! She is just an old crabby woman. Please don't purge me."

Raven turned to the group looking back and forth. "I think we have all we need here. There is no need to place more fear than necessary. These people have already suffered enough."

"Agreed," Ceartas answered. He waved to the young man to indicate he may go. "You have done a great service. We thank you."

The young man left the investigators and headed back to the bakery shop, very briskly.

Dwyn moved away from the group and started heading toward the west side of the square. "Well the day isn't getting any longer, people. Think it's time to see what else we can dig up on this Loach and Norna."

Ceartas followed, as did Raven and Trodaire. When Trodaire caught up to Raven he asked, "Do you think these two people have something to do with this monk's disappearance?"

Raven placed her helmet back on her head. "Not directly."

"How so?" he retorted.

"I'll know more when we talk to these other two, if they are still alive, and I get a good look at the area," she said as she quickened her pace to match Ceartas and Dwyn.

Trodaire chuckled as he also quickened to keep his pace with Raven. “So you’re guessing right now?”

She smirked, “Let’s just say I’m going with women’s intuition.”

“Oh, no. By the Maker, the last time you said that, things got real ugly and Amháin had no choice but to admit he was wrong in front of Aodhfin Bray!” Trodaire exclaimed.

“You were there for that?” Raven asked.

Trodaire nodded.

Dwyn interjected, “The ambush in the Spiral Drachen Pass on the way to Ethens in the Lugos Mountains.”

“It was my first week,” Trodaire remarked.

Ceartas whistled low. “If Raven is correct, we will adjust our tactics accordingly when the time comes. Good thing we are the best at what the Maker has blessed us with in battle and skill.”

“I got a bad feeling about this one, guys,” Trodaire replied.

“I thought you were always up to a challenge, Trodaire?” Dwyn said, snickering.

Raven placed her right arm around the fighter’s shoulders while beginning to enter the west side. “Let’s not worry until we get more information, ok? I could be wrong you know.”

The fighter laughed nervously. “Right and the skies are never blue.”

Ceartas looked skyward. “They are not so blue when rain is near.”

Dwyn added. “There’s some hope she’s wrong then. You know the calm before the storm.”

Trodaire just shook his head as Raven let go of him.

The investigators walked a few blocks and began to see some of the other destruction within the town of Agot. The dwellings were in rows only separated by the dirt passageways or alleys. Various homes and shops throughout the rows followed a slight curve.

Raven noticed that most of the houses were made of wattle and daub, their walls now broken. A fence of pliable hazel sticks wove between many such homes. Blood stains adorned a great many openings. Simple folk died at the entrances of those homes, cut down by a superior foe.

As they entered west side proper, Raven could see that these houses were built with heavily fortified stone. This was the original Agot, before the gable-type houses were added on the east end of town.

Damage appeared thickest here. Raven could see into many buildings. Wooden posts now separated the aisles within the homes, breaking up the living space. Many doorways were smashed inward, while others had been gutted by fires. Blackened char marks danced across smeared window panes.

A few, not many, were burnt completely to the ground. When they entered a small clearing of shops they noticed a small pub called "The Drunken Priest". A half-broken door hung limply on its hinges, and boards were tacked up on the windows. Strangely, there was activity inside.

"Good place as any to make some inquiries," Dwyn stated.

The quartet made their way up to the damaged building. They could hear all the hustle and low murmur of the many patrons and staff before they even crossed the threshold of the doorway, the inquiries of the day's special, asking for more ale, the satisfactory meal or the one meal that was not quite what the customer ordered. When they entered, the room fell silent except for the scrape of a chair or two within the space. The customers looked at the investigators nervously, as if they were waiting for another attack of some sort. It seemed like time slowed, but within a few moments, the customers began one by one picking up where they left off in their previous conversations. Some, however, were watching the small group, suspicious why they were truly there.

Ceartas moved forward toward the main bar-like structure where the owner of the establishment was. Dwyn, Raven and Trodaire followed for a moment then made their way over to a table toward the back, nearest to the kitchen area access. As they were taking their seats, Raven could overhear one of the customers' low exchanges off to her left. She removed her helmet and placed it on the table. "I know, I know, Brackus, this attack was unprecedented. Now we have the Enclave here. What does it all mean?"

Raven glanced over to the left, toward the table where the conversation was coming from. Among the empty wooden cups of ale were two plates of half eaten mutton, potatoes, and carrots. The two large gentlemen sitting took up most of the table themselves. They were dressed in the clothing of the land, possibly farmers or peasants. Their grungy dark brown breeches with various patches and small rips were complimented by their grey shirts, which also bore patches from working fields.

The man on the right began poking at his potatoes and then slightly pointed toward Raven and the group with his fork before getting a potato, placing it in his mouth. She deduced that this was probably Brackus, for he was responding to his comrade's statement while chewing the food. "It means, old friend, that the way of the monks up at that monastery is no more. Look at 'em. Have you ever seen that type of Enclave soldier grouping, other than their leader over there talking to Reidwad?" as he pointed to Ceartas at the counter area again with his fork, before taking his knife and cutting the mutton on his plate. The other man looked right at Raven and averted his eyes quickly. "No, but I think we need to finish and leave. That woman over there can hear us."

Brackus looked directly at Raven, staring with his hazel eyes full of hatred. His long black hair was tied tightly around the back with a large braided ponytail that hung just over his right shoulder. "You have a problem, missy? Isn't any of your business, what we are talking about, so I'd suggest you mind your own, understood?"

Raven was about to make a snide remark when Ceartas came up to the table, diverting her attention from the man snapping at her. "Well that wasn't very helpful," the battle healer stated, and looked at Raven, and the table where the men were, then back at her. "Did I interrupt something, Exactor Raven?" he asked.

Dwyn kicked back his chair on its back two legs and placed his feet on the table, crossing his arms behind his head, balancing himself. "In fact you did. I think Raven was about to teach that guy Brackus over there a lesson." Trodaire just pointed toward Raven and the stout man to their left at the other table.

"Why is that?" Ceartas asked.

There was a shifting of some chairs from the right of the battle healer. A man was trying to calm his friend. "Brackus, no. It's not worth it," another voice from behind Ceartas called out. It was Reidwad, whom he had just talked to moments before. "Brackus, I just got this place presentable."

Ceartas turned to face Brackus, and he was confronted by a burly two hundred seventy pound man standing approximately six inches taller than him. As he looked up to the man he could feel the rancid breath upon his face and the heat of his body.

"Yes, why is that religious bitch going to teach me a lesson? She was eavesdropping on a conversation that was none of her business!" Brackus said with a spray of spittle in Ceartas' direction. The battle healer easily avoided it by taking a step to his right, away from the table. He never took his eyes off the large man.

"Exactor Raven, how would you suggest we rectify this situation in a civil manner without endangering the innocent patrons of this fine establishment?" Ceartas asked as he stared intently into the other man's hazel eyes.

The attention of the two men was interrupted by the sound of armor clasps being undone from the table where the investigative team sat. When they both turned to the table at which Raven was standing, they found her removing her armor's chest- and back-plate from her body.

Raven was proud of her figure, and the exposure of her voluptuous yet firmly-toned upper body in a combat bodice, as usual, did wonders for the slavering men. She placed all her weapons on the floor. Next she put her left leg on the chair and began removing the armor from her dark green breeches. She noticed them staring from her leaning over position, and smirked slightly. "We take this outside gentlemen, so this…" She placed the one leg armor piece on the table and looked Brackus up and down then switched legs and started on the other armor removal, still smirking, "…angry little man can have his honor or vengeance restored as he sees fit. It doesn't matter to me."

Everyone in the establishment was in shock at the smaller warrior woman disarming herself, getting ready to fight someone that had her by at least an arm's length and could pick her up and snap her like a twig. Trodaire looked at Raven with concern in his eyes. "You can't be serious?"

Dwyn, still in his comfortable position, chuckled. "I am sure she will do fine. I'm just wondering how many blows before one of them falls."

Ceartas interjected, "Exactor Raven, this is…is… deplorable. You're supposed to represent the Enclave, the church, and the Maker. How is this act righteous and to aid our cause?"

She placed the last piece of armor on the table and stared back at the battle healer intently. "Did Amháin tell you the Maker requires your particular divine skill that allows you entrance into his presence and redemption of your transgressions for this investigation?" she asked.

"In certain words he did, yes," Ceartas answered.

Raven then made her way around the table and began moving to the main door. When in the doorway, she turned back toward everyone. "I am about to use my divine skill to get the information we need. Are you to question the Maker on how I am going to do this, or judge me because you're not as strong as you thought in his eyes?"

Ceartas sighed and grunted in frustration at the woman. "I personally do not approve of this, for the record."

Brackus shoved past the battle healer. "Allow me to punish her for you, priest!" He moved toward the doorway. Raven smiled wickedly then turned out the door to the outside. When she disappeared out the door, Brackus quickened his pace, and soon Ceartas, Trodaire, and a few patrons moved from their positions to go outside to see this event unfolding before them. Dwyn stayed behind, still in his chair, propped up. "Let me know if she knocks him down in five or less," he called out.

Raven was about to the middle of the small street when she turned around to face the large man coming out of the inn. When he made it to the threshold of the door, she called out to him, "Ok farm boy, and let's see what's got your crotch all in a knot, shall we?"

Brackus exited the doorway along with about half a dozen of the patrons. Ceartas and Trodaire also were within the crowd as they began to disperse along the small porch on the front of the building, moving away from the big man. Raven studied the event, but not looking at the people. Instead she was looking at all the debris scattered all around from the repairs they had been making. She noticed a barrel on the right at the corner in front of the porch, a loose plank on the small awning over the porch above Brackus, then another right under the big man on the porch itself. She smiled and the large man saw it, and pointed right at her, his arm shaking furiously. "I'm going to teach you some manners, bitch!"

Raven burst toward Brackus on the porch, her green eyes and face filled with determination and anger. She yelled back at him, "You're about to find out how much of a bitch I really am!"

Brackus braced himself for the little woman coming at him. He shifted his right leg back, crouching just enough with his left leg that he could grab her when she got in range.

Raven got ten feet from the porch and executed a jump while running. Brackus smiled, knowing that she had miscalculated and would land right into his grasp. Raven, in midflight, went forward into a somersault and positioned herself, landing with both feet on the loose plank on the porch, just under the monstrosity of a man.

Brackus, still smiling at his luck, grabbed her with a hand on each of her shoulders. Then he saw the sparkle of white dots within the air as a pain lit in his lower extremities like fire. He had no choice but to loosen his grip due to the pain. Raven disappeared from his sight.

As he began to try to shake off the burn from below, he tracked the woman to his left, only to see her jump on a barrel and then he heard footfalls on the awning above. Another shadow passed before him and she was back in front of him.

He shook the pain away and growled. Brackus began his lunge, only to see Raven quickly sidestep a large plank that came from nowhere and hit him square center on his face. Again he had stars in his eyes and was dazed for a moment. As he stumbled back he felt something like a noose around his neck and a body behind him on his back. The pressure built, the stars within his vision grew, and he couldn't breathe. Then he heard the woman's whispered voice in his right ear. "When you wake up, farm boy, you better have some answers for us. I wasn't even trying. My preferred method would have been some bolts, an axe, and then my sword. The purist is the only person that is allowing you to live."

Brackus gasped for air. In a last ditch effort he backed up into the door frame to dislodge the woman. He heard a grunt from her, but her grasp only tightened. She whispered again, angry, "Nice try, farm boy. Now you're my bitch. Good night!" Brackus fell to his knees due to the lack of oxygen. He felt more pressure, then a pain in the right side of his neck and passed out.

Raven dropped the large man onto the porch face-down. Everyone was in shock at what they saw. She brushed all the dirt and dust from herself. As she was turning to head back into the inn, Ceartas grabbed her right arm with a look of anger and concern for the man she just attacked. "By the Maker, if you just..."

She shook free of him. With her head down, her green eyes looked up to the battle healer in a seductively devilish manner. "Your faith is the only thing that saved that man today, Ceartas. Consider it a gift for all your hard work. I would suggest when he wakes you get what information we need." She winked and, as she entered the inn, abruptly flipped her reddish brown hair with her hand like nothing happened.

Trodaire approached Ceartas, looking down at the large man on the porch. "Did you know?"

"Know what?" the healer asked.

"That she could do all that?" the fighter replied.

Ceartas began picking up the body to drag back into the inn. Trodaire began to assist, along with a few patrons. As they passed the door into the inn, the owner Reidwad let them know they could take a back room for whatever they needed.

They passed not far from their original table, where Raven was putting her armor back on. Dwyn was counting some coins and placing them in Raven's purse, obviously they had a side bet. "Really? Not even one fist? You just used the building?" he asked in a shocked manner.

She looked right at the healer and the fighter with their cargo in tow, seeing their concern. "Why so serious, guys? That was just to let off a little steam."

Ceartas looked at Trodaire. "I think I understand now why Amháin keeps a close eye on her. Did you see the way she looked at me back there?"

The fighter shifted his grip on the dead weight they were moving. "All I know, purist, is that I heard a rumor she was a Vadőr living in the Shemma at one time."

"A Vadőr? I thought they were more of a mountainous nomadic people. Nothing in common with a large forest or elves," the healer replied.

Trodaire shrugged his shoulders as they went past a hallway to an area where some large rooms were. "It definitely explains how she was able to leap like that. Why she has more close combat weapons."

As they opened a door on the right to a large room, Ceartas responded, "Still doesn't explain why she would have been in the Shemma. It does, however, explain how she knew about a possible attack in the mountain pass." They entered the room with the large man to place him on small bed-type cot. It took both of them, and some patrons, to lift Brackus onto the bed. Dwyn and Raven entered, carrying buckets of water.

Raven was about to close the door when Brackus' friend stopped her. "Please don't hurt him. He really doesn't mean any harm." Raven grabbed the young man and pulled him into the room, shutting the door and locking it.

She turned to the group, looking right at the battle healer and the fighter. "Yes, I am from a Vadőr tribe. As for my business in the Shemma, that is no concern of yours."

"You heard that?" Trodaire asked.

Ceartas held up his hand in a *stop* motion to indicate that the time for getting to know the group was not a priority. "We can talk about this later. Right now we need to pursue this lead Exactor Raven has provided."

Dwyn smiled. "May I?" he asked.

The battle healer nodded to the exactor rogue. Then Dwyn picked up a bucket and tossed the water onto the unconscious Brackus. The man immediately began thrashing and moving his arms and legs like he was in a nightmare. He ended up knocking over the bed and hitting the floor. Brackus stood up abruptly.

As that was happening Trodaire approached Raven, walking behind her to come around to her right side, whispering near each of her ears just under all the noise Brackus was making. "I'm curious what range, and if it's true what they say about Vadőr women--that they can be just as ferocious as the Wilder women."

Brackus stood up to face the group before him. Raven turned her head toward the fighter at a slight angle and smirked. "I am from the Impassable Range and you'll have to be a little more patient about my prowess in battle," she whispered then looked him up and down and added, "But at any time just say the word and I will be more than happy to spar in the practice area." She moved up to Ceartas, still smiling.

Brackus looked at the group before him, trying to evaluate the situation he was in. His companion was there in the back. He immediately took a belligerent tone. "Justin, what the hell, we will be the first to disappear when these religious fanatics decide to purge Agot!"

The battle healer put up both hands in a non-confrontational manner. "Look Brackus, we are not here to purge Agot. We are here to investigate the disappearance of Master Ferric from the monastery. However, based on your behavior and attitude toward us, especially toward one of my exactors, we now must question you on what you know within this town."

Brackus smiled wickedly, folding his arms and leaning back against the wall. He harrumphed, "I know nothing, Jasian heretic. Go back to your walled city, where you judge others without fair council."

Just then another bucket of water assailed Brackus. It came from behind Ceartas and Raven. The big man frantically moved his arms and wiped the water from his head and hair and then the upper part of his clothing. Ceartas turned back to the assailant. Dwyn slowly moved the bucket behind his back. "What? It slipped. Better than beating the man like Raven," the rogue stated.

The purist, frustrated with the situation, finally decided to regain his command. "That is enough!" he barked as he pointed to Dwyn. The battle healer then turned to Raven, still pointing. "By the Maker, you exactors will contain your impulses properly to do this investigation with expediency, efficiency and without any more distress to the inhabitants of Agot. Do I make myself clear?"

There was movement of the bed across the room and Ceartas felt the presence of the large man next to him; now he smelled like a wet dog. Brackus chuckled sinisterly. "So let me get this straight, priest: you, being a devout man of the Maker, so self-controlled and ordered, cannot even contain those you command." He crossed his arms again, taking a step back. "So these exactors are nothing more than thugs used to beat and destroy that which you deem unworthy of your so-called heretical doctrine." He looked each one of them in the eyes. "I think I am feeling distraught, being that I was attacked first, with no regard to my rights"

Ceartas let out a small breath of frustration and closed his eyes. He muttered a small prayer to the Maker to give him strength on the next action he was about to take. He opened his eyes and furiously stared at the big man, his blue eyes aflame with determination of his faith. "Allow me to explain how this works, unsaved one of the Defiler. By the Maker's will, I will get to the bottom of this investigation. I do not care what demons you have against my church, my city, my exactors, or my god. Know this, however: as much as you think of me as a priest, I am a man of battle, forged by conflict. I have seen many such as yourself fall and fail to be claimed, by the Defiler, or whatever other god, without proper forgiveness, calling out for their parents at the end of breath. Test me, Brackus. I know you instigated the fight in your drunkenness with my exactor. I know that the pain has something to do with a woman or family you hold dear. If I am wrong, then you know something else that has to do with Master Ferric or the founders of this town. Please give the Maker a reason for me to unleash his righteousness and justice where it needs to go, and not on a man that has been broken and mad at the circumstances he found himself in."

Brackus looked the battle healer up and down and could see the man was in a battle stance, ready to un-hilt his mace and shield. He even saw the reddish-brown-haired exactor, who took him out in front of the inn take a step back and away from the man before him. The other two were in a protective stance in front of his friend Justin. All seemed to be waiting on who was about to engage, analyzing the situation. Brackus impulsively asked the man before him a question. "Do you have a family, priest?"

"I do, but I haven't seen them in seven winters," Ceartas replied, still in a commanding tone.

Brackus backed up and picked up the bed. He set it upright, turned and sat down. "I did… once. Master Ferric tried to save them, but he was too late." When he looked at Ceartas tears were in his eyes. "I tried, but that wild woman… that wild man… last thing I saw was my dead wife and children. Master Ferric… I don't know what happened to him."

Ceartas stood down from his stance and walked over to the broken man. He sat down next to him, leaned forward and folded his hands between his legs. "That's okay. We will find him. We are heartbroken for your loss Brackus, but why instigate one of my exactors?" the battle healer asked.

"Her eyes," he said angrily.

Raven started to move forward. "My eyes… what the…?" She was stopped by Ceartas with a gesture of his left hand.

Brackus looked right at Raven. "You have the same green wild look she had, that untamable look, the unbridled ferocity of chaos that can't be contained. What is the difference between the Wildmen and the Enclave's exactors? Tell me!" he replied with a tear running down the left side of his face. "I thought if I killed you it would make me feel better. I just wanted the green-eyed nightmare to go away. I needed to get rid of that damn skull helmet that will haunt me till my dying day."

Ceartas stood up and looked at Brackus, then toward his exactors. “Very well Raven, Trodaire, I need you to leave the room, please. Dwyn, I need you to stay here with me and Justin while I converse with Brackus.”

Dwyn was about to protest when the battle healer held up his right index finger. “Do as I instruct. If we are to find Master Ferric, by the Maker we need to heal this man’s wounds properly.” He nodded to Raven and Trodaire to go back to the common room.

And they obeyed.

CHAPTER III

They entered the common room and one of the servants came directly up to them and immediately escorted them to a table. "Please, milord, milady…," a very young girl only about ten to twelve winters age said. "My father wishes to thank you for the non-lethal manner in which you handled Mr. Brackus. Your mid-meal is on the house for you and your group."

Raven smiled at the little girl as she took her seat. "Tell your father he is very welcome and we will welcome his generosity toward the Enclave." Trodaire also sat and added, "Yes, and we will have water with our meals, young miss. Thank you."

"No… no… thank you. My father has so much to do, and you prevented more damage that would set him back another month. I will go fetch your waters and bring your meals soon after," she replied. The two exactors nodded to the little girl, and she went off to get them their orders.

Trodaire focused back on Raven. "So, since we have some time, care to enlighten me on how you were in the Shemma?" he asked innocently.

Raven, her thoughts still on what Brackus had said about the Wildmen attack on his family, didn't hear the fighter's words. All she could think about was *You have the same green wild look she had, that untamable look, the unbridled ferocity of chaos that can't be contained.*

"Raven?" Trodaire asked, noticing her lack of attention.

She quickly shook her head. "I'm sorry. You were saying?"

He laughed. "I didn't think anything would faze you," the fighter stated. "I was asking if you were willing to tell me about the Shemma."

She sighed, but smiled when the little girl brought their water, and thanked her again. When the server left, she turned her chair and faced the fighter. "It was a long time ago, before I was with the Jasian Enclave, and the group that led to the Enclave."

"So you were there… interesting," Trodaire replied.

"How so?" she asked

The fighter smiled. "I had a bet with some of the men in the contingent, when that rumor surfaced, that I could find out."

She laughed, "Really? How much was the pot when you were assigned to this task?"

"Thirty gold coins, at least half a year's pay," he answered.

Raven turned her chair back toward the table. "I should have held out longer and negotiated a cut of the profits."

The fighter laughed, "Oh, so you knew about this. Why I am not surprised. Let me guess: woman's intuition right?"

She nodded. "Yep."

He turned his chair toward her as the food was brought to them and set on the table. He thanked the server and then put his attention back on Raven. "So a long time ago, before your service to the Jasian Enclave… I am curious why a Vadőr from the Impassable Range would be so far from home."

"It's complicated," Raven said as she picked up her wooden cup of water and took a sip. Trodaire could see the fire in her eyes as she said it. Obviously there was something more about this woman's past than her transgressions with a bunch of bandits or the Jasian Enclave. He looked at her for a moment, narrowing his right eye. He moved his chair back to position himself to consume his meal. "Fine… don't tell me. But I will just be a pest until we get this job done." Trodaire picked up his utensils and began to eat.

The two sat there, quietly eating their meal for a few moments. Raven just had another refill of water from the server when she spoke. "I was captured by the slave traders of Malten after a skirmish against my mother's tribe. We were just north of the kingdom of Halsbren and I was a child of no more an age then our proprietor's young daughter that is serving us."

"I take it then you know who or what was responsible for that attack against your tribe?" Trodaire replied as he finished his mutton. He turned back toward her and took a sip from his cup.

"I do, and I would prefer to not proceed with this conversation," she said, turning her head and looking right at him. Her green eyes bore into his.

The fighter turned back to the rest of his meal and drink, speaking to her one last time. "That's fine, Raven. If you could just tell me two things, I'll consider the matter closed."

"What's that?" she asked.

"How did you end up in the Shemma after the traders, and is it true that all Vadőr tribes are a society of women with no men?" he asked.

Raven smiled at the request. She took another bite of food and another drink of water. "There was a large storm that capsized the slave boat on the River Faith near the lake. I ended up near the Shemma, and was taken in by a Goldhym couple with a small child who found me quite feral, near the forest. They were... keepers of knowledge. I learned all I could from them and enhanced my skills in the Shemma. I am what you call in some societies a woodsman. As for the Vadőr tribes, yes, we are a society ruled by women. Do we have men? Yes we do." She stopped and began to finish the rest of her meal.

Trodaire was about to say one more thing when she held up her hand, silencing him. He chuckled and finished his meal. In between his last few bites he retorted, "Wouldn't mind visiting one of those villages someday."

Raven placed her plate and cup off to the side, cleared her throat, and then folded her hands on the table. "Trodaire how can you have such an impure thought being one of the Enclave? What would Amháin do to you for such a thing? Oh and by the way, our men have to earn their right to be by our side in all things." She looked at him, stand-offish. "So far you haven't impressed me."

He was about to answer when Ceartas approached and asked, "Is there anyone that has impressed you, Exactor Raven?"

Without missing a beat, Raven turned her head to the healer, and answered, "Ser Bray"

Dwyn piped in, "Him? Really, why is that?"

"His determination, magnetism, and the red within his hair are all the first qualities' Vadőr women look for in their men," she replied.

Trodaire asked, "First qualities? There are more? And what is the deal about red in the hair?"

Raven sighed. "Red shows strength, fire of the mountain, and ferocity. Many Vadőr women in leadership positions are red-headed. Many of our children are born with the trait, but by the rite of passage some fade to other colors, such as mine."

"So that's why..." the fighter began. But Raven held up her hand, ending his line of thought.

Dwyn spoke up, "Did we miss something?"

Raven changed the subject. "Ceartas, our meals are free for assisting with Brackus. Did you heal the man's wounds, as you put it?"

Ceartas and Dwyn sat down at the table and the little servant girl came at once to give them their food and water. When the food was in front of them the healer said the blessing to the Maker. He then told them their next preparation in between bites and drinks of water. "Thanks to Brackus, we have found out that Loach's place is not far from here. On the way we will be passing Norna's old shop she used to run. We should find some clues at either place. Justin also knew of a rumor that Master Ferric used to know Loach's father. According to both witnesses there was a group of four Wildmen attackers. One apparently was a woman warrior, which is rare. They almost single-handedly did most of the damage we have been seeing, and killed about six to eight townsfolk. It would have been more if not for Master Ferric stepping in. They believe that he may have taken out two would-be assailants, and was pursuing the others."

"If that is the case he may be outside the town limits, and he's been gone a week, too? Only the Maker will know where he is at this point," Trodaire replied.

Raven looked at Ceartas. "Where is Brackus' dwelling from here?"

"About two blocks west," Ceartas answered.

Raven began to prep herself, making sure her armor was tightened. She double-checked her weapons then moved her chair and stood up. The rest of the group watched the woman secure her equipment as if she was going into battle. She looked at them, seeing that Ceartas and Dwyn were still in the middle of their meal. "I'd like to take Trodaire ahead to Brackus' dwelling if you don't mind. It may shed some light on what we may be facing."

Ceartas nodded as he was in the middle of chewing. Dwyn gulped down his water. "Hey, save some action for us," he said before cutting into his mutton.

The fighter secured his gear and briefly looked at Dwyn. "Don't worry, my friend. I am sure we will find nothing but debris." He walked past Raven and slapped her on the shoulder. "Shall we?" he asked. Raven shook her head and followed.

After Raven and Trodaire left the inn they headed west, further into the town. Along the way they confirmed with a citizen the directions to Brackus' home to verify they were heading the right way. The two exactors' didn't speak. Their focus was on getting to their destination.

When they made it to the area in question, they could see the damage from the battle. There was debris everywhere, including planks in the street and shards of glass that had yet to be cleaned. Brackus' home was in shambles. The only thing that was left to identify it was the small family sign lying off what would have been the porch front stairs. The dwelling that was once a heavily-fortified stone and wooden rampart building now was a pile of burnt rubble.

Each home on either side was also damaged. It seemed that whatever hit Brackus' home hit all three at the same time. Trodaire whistled low, "Last time I saw damage like this it was done by a so- called sorcerer, nasty work."

Raven began looking at the loose dirt all around, trying to find the imprints of any recent footfalls that would create a walled-type depression. Moving slowly and precisely, she paced in a circle at times in some particular spots. She checked the areas around the fronts of all the homes. She even went into some of the devastated homes.

Some townsfolk approached, curious about what she was doing. Raven motioned to Trodaire to intercept them so as not to disturb her investigating the grounds. She could tell over the past week there were many tracks that had contaminated the area. She began concentrating on the largest of distortions. Raven separated between the many overall tracks and possible true tracks she was looking for. She knew if that if she read the area wrong, the actual targets her group was looking for, would be lost. During the investigation of the area, she noticed something strange. There were various scorch marks here and there which should have been nearer to the buildings. They were on the ground, like fire was thrown in different directions at the suspected Wilders.

She was well into her routine for a good five minutes when Ceartas and Dwyn caught up to them. The healer and rogue could see that Trodaire was doing what he could to contain the small crowd that gathered, wondering why a group of purists were in their neighborhood. Ceartas nodded to Dwyn to go assist the fighter. He then looked at the area, noticing how close they were from the edge of the town, closer to the farm land and foothills. He noticed that Raven was crouched down so he called out to her, "Anything interesting, Exactor Raven?"

She stood up and approached the battle healer, and then whistled for the others. Trodaire and Dwyn left the townsfolk to allow them to go about their business. When they all gathered, Raven indicated to them to walk with her toward Brackus' dwelling. She spoke in a low tone, just above a whisper. "There were four in the beginning, just as Brackus and Justin said. One fell here." She pointed to an area off to their right, about ten feet away from the porch. "Two were in combat with our missing monk."

"And the fourth?" Ceartas asked.

Raven gave Trodaire a look that he had seen once before. "Oh by the... I was right about something, wasn't I?" he stated.

She looked back to Ceartas, "Magic was used here."

"Ambrosia?" Dwyn asked.

The battle healer's face grew dark with concern. "It fits the description. A female with Wildmen, wild eyes, and now magic. We may have to get the rest of the contingent and inform Purist Amháin."

"No...there's something else," Raven interjected, "besides the strange fire strikes at the Wilders on the grounds here."

"What?" Trodaire asked.

Raven pointed over to where the one Wildman had fallen. "There was a set of snake-type tracks that burrowed into the ground. I have seen snake holes, but never like this or with that type of tunneling."

Dwyn grimaced. "Small snakes that burrow into solid ground? I thought they were bigger and in certain areas, not around here."

"Ceartas, which way is the alchemist's and founder's dwellings?" Raven asked.

The battle healer pointed to the southwest. "It's about another block over and maybe five or six buildings that way. Why?"

Raven looked in that direction and then toward the empty space of the farm and hilly area more to the west. She relied on her training from her adopted brethren, the Elves. "There were also two other pairs of footprints, not belonging to Wilders. One seemed to be limited, almost lame. You can tell by the slight scraping of the ground. What is strange about it is that the tracks moved in a pattern of a normal faster-paced individual with no injury to support the wound. Many with that type of wound, the scraping would be at least two to three times larger. The other was small strides with petite depressions, maybe an Elf could make these but I have not seen any other Elves in town. The logical conclusion would be a tiny woman or a child. Both seemed to have engaged the Wildmen along with the monk. They retreated back toward the direction you indicated, with a single Wilder giving chase. Two Wildmen took off running due west, with the monk in pursuit. Dwyn looked at Raven. "Why would a Wildman not engage the bigger threat of Master Ferric, but instead go after two others? It isn't their style or tactics."

"The alchemist shop!" Raven exclaimed, snapping her fingers.

Ceartas looked at the woman and began pointing right at her. "We have one of two possibilities. One, it's Ambrosia going to go get components to keep her power over the Wildmen; or two, one of her trusted fighters went to get the components for her."

Trodaire added, "Begging your pardon, Ser, but an alchemist doesn't have magic. They deal in chemical compositions with solids and liquids."

"No, they also carry magical components to enhance those items. I also know some may have limited spell creation just as so-called Creationists." Dwyn answered.

Ceartas looked at the members of his team individually with a determination of being battle ready. "We need to find out what has been taken from that shop. This way we have an idea of what to expect from our enemies when we go to engage them. Let's move exactors. Time is already against us."

They quickly ran down the street, then turned right and moved west to the next block over. When they came to the shop of the alchemist, Norna Dewin, it was oddly intact with no signs of damage. Ceartas stopped short and held his group back with a move of his arms on either side of him. "This isn't right. Do we have the right place?"

Dwyn pointed up by the awning on the porch. "Yep, there is the sign." The notice was in an oak frame with hickory back, which was painted in white markings. "Dewin's Spiritual Concoctions and Goods".

"Raven, tracks, I want to know who came here and where they've gone. Dwyn, I need you to go check up there cautiously, and then make your way toward the back. I don't like this," Ceartas commanded.

The rogue smiled and almost skipped as he moved forward. "On it boss. I'll make sure we don't trip anything as small as a spider web." He slowed when he was near the porch. About ten feet out he searched where he was safe to step.

"Trodaire, I want you to go over to the building to the right, and from behind make your way to the back with Dwyn. Understood?" the battle healer ordered. The fighter nodded and then moved.

Ceartas whispered a small prayer for victory and protection for his exactors and moved forward toward the small shop. As he was about halfway to his destination, Dwyn gave a thumbs-up for the area then pointed to the door and indicated it had some possible damage. The rogue began his journey to the back, going to the opposite side of the building Trodaire did.

Ceartas made it to the bottom of the stairs, stopped, and closed his eyes. "Exactor Raven, I need an assessment please."

Raven walked up next to him and whispered toward his right ear. "All three tracks lead here. The tracks indicate the small one first, then the lame one, lastly the Wildman. All of them entered from this direction. No exit tracks at all, unless they left out the back." She looked around quickly to see if anyone was watching them. "All is clear so far out here. Should I cover you at range?"

Ceartas seemed to be in some form of meditation, taking Raven's words in. He opened his eyes. "No, prepare for CQC. I don't want anyone to even have the opportunity to escape this dwelling. Understood?"

Raven nodded. "Shall we?" she asked as she untied her throwing axe for easy access.

The two warriors slowly went up the small stairs, hands on their weapons as they approached the door. They immediately noticed that it had once been off its hinges but was very recently repaired. Ceartas was about to try the door handle when they heard a "Psst...," from their right. They looked and it was Dwyn. He whispered to them, "All clear, nothing but a bunch of smelly, dead-stinking trash with glass, wood and things I don't recognize."

Ceartas nodded, and instructed using hand signals, "Sneak in the back." Dwyn nodded and disappeared back around the corner. The battle healer focused on the door handle and found it unlocked. He and Raven opened the door and entered.

A small bell over the door rang as they entered. They heard a young voice call from the back of the four large, shelved isles of bottles. "Afternoon. Please... please... come in, come in. What can old Norna or I do for you?"

Cautiously, Ceartas and Raven moved forward, still with their hands on their weapons. The battle healer was concentrating on the young woman at the counter. Raven happened to glance at the shelving and noticed it was all new construction and stocked with new bottles. She coughed to get Ceartas' attention. When he looked she nodded to the shelves. He returned the nod and pressed forward.

The shop had various jars and bottles filled with many differently colored liquids and substances and items such as fingernails, or bear's claws. Raven even thought she saw the eyeballs of some type of animal. The place smelled like fresh vanilla with lilac.

As they closed in on the counter they could see a young woman in a grey and blue flower-patterned sun dress. She had a small leather belt with a pouch. Her back was to them while she stood on a stool putting away a few jars on a large shelving cabinet behind the counter. Her blonde hair glistened in the sunlight provided by the four windows of the shop. She came down off the stool and turned around to face the duo. Her bright blue eyes sparkled with happiness. She couldn't be more than about twenty winters old. She was small-framed but average in figure. She reached over to her pouch and pulled out a small flask, then took a sip and put it back. She asked them, "How can I help you today?"

Ceartas, still holding his hand on his weapon replied, "We would like to talk to Norna, please. It's about Ser Hynafin."

The girl's eyes widened. "Oh, my, has he run out of his medicine again?"

"Med...," Ceartas was about to ask, when Raven grabbed his right arm and interrupted. "Yes, seems he is going through a lot of it due to the attack over a week ago."

"I see. Well let me get the extra Norna made for him," she said as she moved behind the counter area, toward the back and into the storage area through a small doorway. As soon as she disappeared Raven and Ceartas heard the footfalls of someone running. When they realized it was the young girl, they gave chase. Right after they entered the back area, they could hear her yelling, "No... no!" Just past the rows of shelving, in a more open area, was a huge table with a large fabric tarp on top of something. On the other side, just beyond it, was the back door. Holding the young woman was Dwyn and Trodaire. The fighter smiled as he escorted the woman back. "Lose something, Ceartas?" he asked as he pushed her forward toward the battle healer.

Raven noticed that the area was highly scented with various candles, incense, oils, and assortments of dried petals and spices in various bowls and urns all over. She took a deep breath through her nose and found another fragrance: death and rot.

"I didn't do anything! Let me go!" the young woman yelled.

Ceartas looked at her intently. "Then why did you run?" he asked sternly.

Raven slowly moved toward the table as the group at the other end questioned the girl. The odor was getting stronger there. She noticed dried blood stains on the floor and on the bottom of the tarp at the corners.

"I was told by Norna if anyone came looking for Ser Hynafin I was to go to his home and wait until she returned," the young frightened woman replied.

Raven then saw a large protrusion off on the right side like something holding the tarp off the table. She slowly approached it and started to look at it more closely.

Trodaire interjected, "Why would she have you go there?"

The woman looking at the group saw Raven getting closer to the tarp on the table. She quickly answered frantically, "She said it would be the only place I would be safe...," Raven was beginning to reach down to the side of the tarp. "No! Don't touch that!" the woman cried out.

Raven pulled back the piece and saw a large hand in a clawed position. She immediately grabbed the rest of the tarp and moved it off the table. The young woman screamed out, "No! You will release the plague!" and tried to free herself from the fighter.

On the table was a Wildman in a slow state of decomposition. His legs were gone, sawed off in order to fit him on the table. Raven guessed he would have been about seven feet. All he had on him was some skins and furs, virtually no armor on him. His chest was exploded open, the breast plate broken in half, exposing the internal organs. Dwyn moved off to the side and threw up his lunch next to the back door. Trodaire almost loosened his grip on the woman, but held fast. Ceartas had nothing to say but, "By the Maker…,"

Raven walked around the table and approached the woman, pointing to the body. "What happened here?"

"You have to cover the body or the plague will be released!" she cried wildly.

"A cover on a body does not prevent a plague," Raven answered.

She shakily started to point toward the shelf next to the table. "But the creatures will come and take us over," she replied.

Raven followed the direction and made her way over to the shelf in question. Ceartas moved over toward the young woman. "Who is this Wildman?" he demanded.

"He was the shaman. He destroyed Brackus' home with fire from his hands. That's what Norna said," the woman answered.

Dwyn, recovering from his slight sickness, said, "Wildmen don't use magic; they hate it."

Trodaire released the woman to Ceartas. "Yet they follow Ambrosia, who is a sorceress."

Raven, once over at the shelf, noticed various labeled elixirs and salves for many things: health, rejuvenation, and then one that she recognized for another purpose. She quickly checked if the others were paying attention- especially Dwyn. They were so involved with the woman they were not looking at Raven. She quickly took the small bottle, ripped off the label and placed it in her traveling pouch. When she looked up she saw something she had never seen before. The creature in the large jar was about twelve inches in length and just bigger in diameter than an arrow shaft. She could see a trisecting jawed mouth, frozen in mid-opening. She could also see what looked like undeveloped wings fused on the side of its body structure. It had the characteristics of a small snake. She picked up the jar and faced the group with it. “It's quite dead, but I have never seen anything like it.” She handed it over to Trodaire.

He looked at it then handed it to Dwyn. “What is it” he asked, looking back at the woman.

Dwyn shook as if he had a shiver pass through his body, and then put the jar on the table next to the body. “That came out of him?” he asked.

The woman quickly answered, “He followed Norna and Ser Hynafin here to the shop. I was in the back when everything was being destroyed. Norna managed to subdue him with one of her gaseous elixirs, and Ser Hynafin cut him down. It was when they brought him back here...” she pointed to the jar. “...that thing came out of his chest and made a Maker awful noise. I couldn't move, nor could Hynafin. Norna was the only one that could move because she is mostly deaf. She took one look at it, grabbed her dagger and sliced it in half then placed it in the jar. After that we did our best to clean the shop up all week, but she wanted to study the Wildman. When she heard that Master Ferric had gone missing, she told me to stay here and trust no one. If anyone came asking for her or Ser Hynafin I was to go to his place until she returned and she knew it was safe.”

Ceartas placed his hand on his forehead and with his index and thumb and rubbed his brow. “So let me get this straight. Three Wildmen, one being a woman, continued to attack the monk, a deaf woman and a lame but capable fighter. Things go bad and two leave with the Monk in pursuit while this one...” the healer pointed to the dead body, “...has magical powers and goes after the deaf and lame targets only to be taken out by them, and is infected by some worm or snake creature? Then when the rumor surfaces that the monk is missing, these same two individuals go to save Master Ferric?” He looked at the young woman. “Young lady, I think there is more about your employer than you're telling us. I would suggest you come clean. I am not about to have my exactors engage this wild woman who may be a powerful sorceress.”

The woman began to cry, “How do I know I can trust you? Norna said I could only trust her.”

Raven walked up to Ceartas and placed her right hand on his shoulder. “Let me handle this,” she said quietly.

Ceartas nodded and then turned to the others. “Let's get this poor bastard out of here and give him a proper burial. I am sure the rest of him is outside in that garbage." Trodaire and Dwyn nodded and opened the back door and then went to get the body moved while the healer began a prayer ritual.

Dwyn spoke up. "Ceartas, can you extract the final thoughts of those that have passed?" The battle healer nodded while not breaking the chant or ritual.

Trodaire grabbed one end of the body while Dwyn had the other. The fighter added, "That's what he's going to do while we bury this guy, so we can get more information." They moved the body out the door of the shop.

When the men left, Raven led the young lady by the hand and took her back to the front of the store. "We are not here to harm you, Norna, or Ser Hynafin. We are investigating the disappearance of Master Ferric. Any information you have that can help us understand why he has not returned or why there is a relationship with Norna and Hynafin would be a great help. The Order needs him back soon. They are lost without his guidance. Do you understand?"

The young woman nodded, "Yes."

Once in the front part of the store, Raven placed the young woman back behind the counter and she took a seat on one of the stools there opposite her. She folded her hands in front of her and asked, "How about you tell me what happened here when that Wilder showed up."

The young lady took a deep breath, closed her eyes and then looked at Raven. "I was in the back gathering all the healing agents I could for the town, when I heard Norna and Hynafin come running in. It couldn't have been more than a few seconds when I heard the front door coming off the hinges and smashing into the first shelf. I slowly began to move to the front when I heard the Wildman scream at Norna, something about he thought she was dead hundreds of winters ago and she would not escape him. When I looked around the corner Norna threw three bottles, and a cloud formed and engulfed the Wildman. When it cleared, the attacker was frozen in place and Hynafin ran his sword through his chest, killing him."

Raven blinked at the woman then asked, "What did he mean by her being so old, and how is that related to Ser Hynafin and Master Ferric?"

The young woman reached over and grabbed her flask and took another drink from it. When she put it back she looked at Raven. "She knows a lot of old history, but has no books here about it. Norna also knows things about components and elixirs that can extend one's life."

"So what, you're older than you look?" Raven inquired.

"I am forty-one winters old," the young woman answered. She didn't look a day over twenty.

Raven looked around the shop. "So some of the things I have seen here are what Dwyn told us. It's a store with a gathering of many different things that also have magical properties?" She slowly reached down without the young woman noticing and tapped the pouch that had the vial she grabbed earlier.

The woman nodded. "I am Norna's apprentice, Maggie."

"So what is the connection between Hynafin and Ferric?" Raven again asked.

"The founder was on an adventure with his father and Master Ferric many winters ago when he was wounded with a crippling injury, never to walk again. Ser Hynafin's father was killed and before passing made Master Ferric promise to keep an eye on him from a distance," Maggie replied.

Raven stood up. "So they made it here to Agot when it was a hamlet and met Norna."

Maggie nodded. "She gave him medicine to help him walk again, but over the winters it has been wearing off more and more. Master Ferric joined the Order at the monastery soon after and became one of the masters. Over the last twenty winters Agot grew to what we have today."

"Thank you, Maggie. You have been helpful, now we just have to find out why they went to assist Master Ferric," Raven said. She stood and started to make her way toward the back door to the others.

Ceartas met her in the doorway to the back storage area and stopped her. "Norna thinks Master Ferric is in danger and will not survive the other two Wildmen."

Raven just blinked at the healer. "Why do you think that?" she asked.

"During the extraction of information from the dead Wildman, I found that he was not in control of himself." Ceartas seemed shaken. "Apparently he knew things of an ancient nature and Norna is not what she seems. Someone or something assisted another person called Shanti, which this entity, or demon, hated."

"Are you alright?" Raven asked, concerned.

Ceartas composed himself and looked at Raven with a divine determination. "I am concerned for Ser Bray, and pray that the Maker will protect him. We need to go assist Norna and Hynafin. Luckily the Wilder here was the only magic they had. However, if there are more of those snake demons I fear for all who engage those Wildmen. This whole thing could have been a trap, for all we know. It will take too long to gather the contingent. We must move promptly and with haste, for I fear we may be already too late for Master Ferric."

Raven walked up to him and placed her hand on his shoulder. "I have an idea which direction they went. I can find them," she said as she looked sternly in his eyes.

The two moved out the back of the store toward the other exactors, who were finishing up the covering of the grave they just made for the Wildman. They made sure it was far enough away from the town not to be disturbed, near a small oak tree sapling. When they approached Dwyn, he asked, "So I take it we are off to find this vagabond group?" Ceartas just nodded. Trodaire picked up the shovels and began walking back to put them where they borrowed them from. "Be right back, don't start without me," he said, smiling.

Raven could see the concern on Ceartas' face. The man seemed troubled about the events that had just transpired within Agot. She again tried to reassure him. "This won't take long, trust me. I have a good idea where to start tracking."

Dwyn, seeing Trodaire returning, said, "Well, guess you should begin. We only have about seven hours before it gets dark and you lose the trail."

As the fighter rejoined the group, Raven looked at the leather- bound companion and smirked. "Just because it gets dark doesn't mean I still can't track."

Ceartas took a deep breath, and then said a small prayer. Once done he looked at his comrades. "Very well, let us be off. It's time to find this monk of the Sacred Fist and return him to where he belongs." The group nodded and began their journey back toward Brackus' house to pick up the trail of their adversaries.

It didn't take long to get to the start of the trail. Within the hour the group was heading out into the foothills of the Agontill Highlands. The rolling grassy hills and valleys of the foothills consisted of rich plant life with large areas of small wetlands and rich grass toward the steppes of the Impassable Range not far in the distance. The foothills were drained by small creek beds that filtered toward or near Agot and The

Wilds. They also contained outlying disconnected areas, such as valleys, where many farmers were cultivating the lands or herding animals.

Raven was grateful for the moderate climate of the region. It reminded her of her home, so close now she could almost touch it. She admired various pleasant woodlands here and there in some of the valleys, especially toward the mountains, towards her home.

Raven was at point about a good hundred feet or so, with Dwyn approximately fifty feet behind her. She was again looking at the terrain all around trying to find the slopes, at the base of the tall grass, or small dirt paths, for any recent footfalls that would have created a walled-type depression. She was tracking the Wildmen and Master Ferric's footfalls. The journey was slow and steady. They only rested twice, taking in food rations or drinks of water. After three hours in the foothills, Raven noticed that the tracks turned toward the south, towards The Wilds. It was here that Master Ferric's rescuers were now added in to the mix.

She heard a whistle, like a small bird trilling. Raven looked back and saw Dwyn pointing ahead of her and up toward the sky. When she looked to the direction indicated, she found scavenger birds circling the clear blue sky. She turned back to the thief and nodded, then continued forward.

It was another two hours later when Raven crested the rise of a hill and saw a slaughter below. She immediately dropped down and hid herself amongst the tall grass. The tracker indicated to Dwyn with a quick wave of her arm behind her that there was danger up ahead. He dropped to a crouching position and gave the bird call back to the others. They immediately drew their weapons and crouched down as well.

Raven figured that in five hours they had easily traversed at least twelve miles west to southwest of Agot. The exactors were efficient. She'd hoped to make it in a single day, but she hadn't been sure. It looked like their luck had held. Slowly she lifted her head, using the grass to conceal her, to look at the scene below.

A large stone cottage with a thatch roof was below, and still intact. There was a wooden barn off to the left that was also unharmed. What was disturbing was that all of the animals from the barn were all slaughtered in the open area outside, including the inhabitants of the small plot of land. Off to the right was a third stone building and another set of bodies. Scavenger birds were all about, picking and fighting amongst themselves for any piece of the carcasses they could bite into. Raven about jumped up when she heard Dwyn whisper next to her. "What is that over by the stone building, a large lizard?" he asked.

"I'm not sure from this distance, but it kind of looks like a drachen, what I would guess you now call a dragon in civilized areas." Raven whispered quietly.

"Dragon! Holy hells, I didn't think I'd ever see one in person. I don't see its head. Matter of fact, I don't see any heads on any of those corpses," Dwyn answered, his voice growing tense.

Raven could hear the other companions approaching from behind. They were about a good ten feet from her and Dwyn when Ceartas whispered loudly, "What do you have?"

Raven slowly moved away from the edge of the hill and away from any view point from below to converse with the team. Dwyn followed soon after so as not to give away their position. As she approached she quickly looked behind her to make sure Dwyn was not far. She looked at Ceartas. "The tracks lead down to a farm. Everything is dead down there, based on what I can see from here. I won't know any more until I get down there. I don't know if the Wildmen or the monk is still there," she said as she approached him. Dwyn spoke up while taking Raven's left side. "Raven thinks there is a possible dead dragon down there as well, guys! I think that bad feeling you had, Trodaire, is about to come into play."

Ceartas' brow darkened at the sound of that. "A dragon? No one has seen a dragon in centuries. Are you certain?" he asked.

Raven quickly replied, "I'm not sure, but based on my studies back in the Shemma with my foster family, it looks like it may be. By the look of it from this distance it's huge, about fifteen feet long. I've never seen a lizard so large."

Trodaire's face grew discouraged for a moment, and then he took a deep breath. When he composed himself he said, "A lot of nasty creatures live in the Wilds. Maybe this big nasty wandered out. The only way we are going to find out what it is, is to get down there.

"I don't like the fact that these Wildmen can take out something that large. If that is the case, what hope do we have for Master Ferric?"

Raven looked at the group. "Maybe none, either way we have to find out. Maybe he escaped when the large lizard showed up." She looked at the healer. "What's the plan?"

"Is there any other way down to the farm than this hill?" Ceartas asked.

Raven pointed to his left. "If you go that way you can go down and re-approach as if coming from a path to the farm."

The healer nodded. "Ok, Trodaire and I will take that route and draw anyone watching the main path to us." He looked at Raven. "Is there another path that way?" he asked, pointing to his right. Raven nodded. "Yes, it will come up behind the storage building."

He pointed to Dwyn. "You go the opposite side of us and see if you can approach from that building to the main house." Dwyn nodded and moved to start his portion of the plan.

The healer looked at Raven again. "You position yourself up here with range and hit anyone that attacks us. Understood?" he commanded. Raven nodded and slowly moved back to her position at the top of the hill. She crunched down and hid within the tall grass. Ceartas and Trodaire moved off to start the plan of action.

Raven slowly removed her repeating crossbow from her back and began looking for a way down without being seen. The tall grass was good cover but not close enough range for what she wanted to do. She scanned the area and found a few large boulders imbedded into the hillside toward the farm. She looked for the least possible way to be seen to each of the three boulders she could use. She crawled to the first boulder about twenty-five feet down from the top of the hundred-foot hill and took a quick look. She could see Ceartas and Trodaire just coming around the bend toward the barn. She then looked back to the storage building, and still didn't see Dwyn. She quickly and quietly went low again and started crawling toward the second boulder on the hill, about halfway down. When she reached it she got up with her back against it and quickly looked around the obstacle for another look at where her team was.

She saw the healer and the fighter amongst the dead carcasses, chasing away the birds, looking for survivors. They were constantly looking toward the house to be on their guard should anyone come at them. She caught a glimpse of Dwyn behind the main house in the back. He waited until she made eye contact, and he nodded and darted toward the house.

Raven then, for the third time, crouched down and moved to her final destination of the third rock formation, bringing her twenty-five feet from the base of the tall hill. Once there she positioned herself with cover and found a niche from which she could fire on any opponent. No sooner did she hunker down, when all hell broke loose.

There was screaming from within the house, a scream like a battle cry. Next thing everyone heard was crashing and thuds throughout the home. Then there was the breaking of glass as a body barely made it out through one of the main windows on the right side of the stone structure. The body did a forward tuck and rolled in a somersault, then to its right, and stopped on its back. It was Dwyn, and he was bleeding from multiple wounds in his chest.

Ceartas and Trodaire immediately moved to his side. The fighter took a defensive position with his sword out and the healer tried his best to begin healing the man on the ground.

Two Wilders exited the home in frenzy. One was seven feet tall and about three feet wide, saber-tooth tiger skulls adorned his hands and a basilisk's skull was on his head. The hardened muscles of his arms were holding a massive axe. His bare chest was covered in blood still streaming from up by his neck. The second one was seven-and- a-half-feet tall and three-and-a-half-feet wide, and definitely female. She was sporting leather and fur that covered her large muscular frame and minute bosoms in a battle bodice of reinforced snakeskin. Her shoulders each had basilisks' skulls on both sides. On her head, fresh still with pockets of scales on the skull, was the horned frame of a lizard. This Wilder also had bone- plated legs and forearms with saber-tooth skulls on both hands. She held two axes without effort.

The smaller Wildman ran up toward Trodaire and began swinging his axe with such brutal effectiveness the fighter had no choice but to parry every blow. Raven watched as each impact weakened the fighter's arms against the mighty strength of the larger man. The woman just watched, licking her lips and waiting for something. Another blow sent the fighter off to one side, exposing his left flank. The Wildman countered again and sliced deep into Trodaire. Raven concentrated, focused her sight and steadied her aim. As Trodaire collapsed on his knees to the ground, the Wildman spun around to cleave the head off the fighter. Raven exhaled and squeezed the trigger.

Five bolts found themselves center mass of the smaller Wildman, piercing his heart. The warrior stumbled back in shock, bewildered as he looked down at the feathery protrusions. He then fell to the ground, dead. Raven quickly reached behind her into her pack and grabbed another container of bolt arrows. She hit the quick release on the crossbow, dropping the empty one.

The female Wildman screamed a battle cry as drool and foam cascaded from her mouth from under the hideous skull. Her green eyes were aflame with hatred at what just transpired. She leaped from the doorway, swinging both axes in a forward motion like a saw about to cut wood. She was running right at Trodaire to mow him down. Her speed was impressive. Raven was trying to reconnect the container to fire again but knew that she would not get it in time to save the fighter.

Then there was a loud clash of metal as Raven connected the container in its place. She immediately repositioned herself in a firing stance in time to see Ceartas knocking the woman off her target with his shield. This just infuriated the Wild Woman more, as she missed the still-kneeling Trodaire only by inches with her axe blade.

Raven took aim as the woman spun around to engage the battle healer. She was about to do another center mass when Ceartas got in the way. She quickly re-adjusted to her target's obstacle and fired.

Ceartas came up quickly to put distance between him and Trodaire from the wild woman. He placed his shield to guard him against the woman. He was taking his battle mace and swinging from the right when he heard five wisps of air go by him. He connected with the mace into the woman's lower jaw, knocking her back about five feet. Then he saw the bolts. One in her upper right thigh, one in each of her shoulders, the fourth in her left upper thigh. The Wild Woman was no longer wearing her dragon skull.

Her braided hair, all matted in caked blood, came tightly to her large forehead decorated in multiple tribal tattoos. Her fierce green eyes were enhanced with blackened outlines. Ceartas was certain that the Defiler himself was in possession of the humanoid beast of a woman. She seemed to be re-assessing her position, looking at the arrows in her body. She then let go of her axes and let them drop to the leather straps tied to her wrists. She charged Ceartas. He braced himself with his shield in front of him for the impact.

Raven saw the woman run up and instead of bashing the battle healer, she grabbed his entire body, shield and all. The Vadőr woman knew he would not last long. She quickly studied the area, noticing any footing that would give her the high ground, and reloaded her final arrow bolt container to her crossbow, loosening her armor straps. An idea came to her and she hesitated only a moment before she reached into the pouch that contained the vial she took from the alchemist's shop. She opened the bottle and pulled her longsword. Raven swiftly added a few drops of the substance onto the blade, and then re-sheathed her sword. She closed the bottle and put it back in her pouch. When she looked around the cover of the boulder she saw Ceartas being squeezed. The Wild Woman slammed her own skull into his.

Once.

Twice.

Three times.

She let go and Ceartas dropped to the ground.

The Wild Woman backed up and smiled wickedly with her crooked teeth as she slowly placed her axes back into her hands. Confident in her victory, she walked over to Trodaire and kicked him to the ground. The Wilder brought her axe up high.

When she was at her pinnacle, ready to descend, Raven moved from her position and began firing. The five arrows pierced into the Wild Woman, but not a single shot hit center mass. When Raven got to the edge of the farm she dropped the crossbow and took her throwing axe to cut her other straps to her armor, letting it fall as well.

The Wild Woman, now with a total of nine bolt arrows in her, again smiled wickedly. "So this is the best the Jasian Enclave has to offer?" she asked sarcastically. She was still unfazed by the arrows protruding from her body.

Raven looked at the men on the ground, and then returned a smirk back to the barbarous woman. "No, they are just men; no match for a woman's wrath or revenge," she answered.

"You are a cowardly female, using range weapons thinking you can defeat me. I will kill you just for sport," the Wild Woman said, bringing up her axes in a defensive posture.

Raven smiled just as wickedly as her opponent did. "I wouldn't have it any other way, bitch. I have been waiting for a rematch with your kind since I was thirteen winters-old."

The two ran at each other with tremendous speed. The Wild Woman had reach with her axes over Raven, but that didn't stop the Vadőr. Right when she came within the reach of her rival, Raven immediately dropped to her knees, sliding on the loose ground just under the swings of the two axes aimed for her head. Pulling her throwing axe in mid-slide, Raven cut the leather strap on the left axe, and then sliced into the left upper groin area, passing through the Wild Woman's legs.

The Wild Woman barely let out a grunt as she quickly turned with her right axe and came down toward Raven's back. The Vadőr was quick, but not fast enough. Raven felt the burn of fire down her right side, and her grip weakened on her throwing axe. She immediately leaped forward out of range as the second axe caught a few loose hairs from behind. She turned around to see the large woman advancing. The Vadőr quickly scanned her surroundings and saw what she needed to do.

Raven ran toward the Wilder, switching her throwing axe from right to left. Right before the swing from her opponent she leapt on top of a barrel in a forward somersault over the monstrosity of a woman, and then she tucked and rolled to the right and threw the axe into her back.

With the axe still planted in her back, the wild lady turned around to see Raven standing with her arms and legs apart, looking at her with fierce determination in her green eyes, her hair, cut free, billowing in the highland breeze. The Wild Woman saw the glint of red strands in the dusk of the sun going down.

"A Vadőr, I understand now," she said with a nod. "This is good. When I kill you I will bring back your head and become supreme huntress," the feral female said confidently.

Raven smirked, "Not today." She ran forward toward the woman.

The Wild Woman, right before Raven tried to use the barrel again, smashed it with both her axes. The Vadőr slid around her opponent, jumped up, and grabbed the throwing axe out of her back. Raven then twisted to her left and plunged the axe into the right wrist, severing the leather strap and breaking the hand covering. Muscles severed, the feral woman dropped the great axe.

Enraged, she slammed her fist into Raven, knocking her backwards. Feral and rabid, she pulled the axe out of her arm and threw it away from her.

She grabbed the remaining great axe with both hands, though her grip was weak. Still, she took advantage of the dazed Vadőr. She swung toward Raven.

Raven felt the burning across her abdomen and then more pain in the bottom of her jaw as she was knocked back against the stone house. Stars danced in her eyes as her lungs burned for lost breath. Then she felt something large around her neck. She heard the large woman before she saw her. "Now you will die, Vadőr bitch. But first you will know agony."

As Raven was starting to black out she frantically reached for her longsword. The Wild Woman saw her and smiled. "You want to stab me with your stick?" She moved back and extended her arm, still clutching Raven's throat, squeezing tighter. "Go ahead, it will be the last thing you see, me standing as you die."

The Jasian exactor mustered what strength she had left and unsheathed the sword and in one fluid motion, she spun the sword and cut around her adversary's arm three times. The sword fell from her hands. Raven saw the other woman laugh.

"It's time to die, little bitch," she said, then placed the axe into her wound and began to press while tightening her grip around the throat.

All of a sudden, the pressure stopped and the woman before her fell to the ground. Raven coughed a few times. She was still losing blood and was light-headed. She looked down at the large woman, who still awake but not moving. Raven slowly picked her sword off the ground as she stumbled, then stood over the fallen form and weakly smiled. "Oh… you … don't… know what's happening," she taunted. "This is how you die."

Raven took the sword and slit the woman's throat and then shoved it into wild woman's left eye socket, all the way to the back of her skull, killing her.

She stepped forward, intent on giving help to her comrades, but her legs could not hold her. Her world tilted as she fell to the ground in front of the door of the farm house. And then Raven knew no more.

EPILOGUE

When Raven woke up she found herself lying on a bed in the healing tent of the contingent. She struggled to sit up when one of the female nurses approached. "Milady, please... you must rest." She paid no mind to her and sat up, grunting at the pain in her abdomen.

"So I see that our exactor is up and well," a familiar voice called from the entrance flap of the tent. It was Ceartas, in his now clean armor. He was sporting a small three inch scar on the upper right side of his temple.

Raven gave a slight smile, trying to hide the pain she was in as she adjusted to get more comfortable. "How long?" she asked in between breaths.

"A week," the battle healer answered.

"The others?" she asked a little more comfortable.

Ceartas entered the tent and approached Raven. He grabbed a small wooden chair and placed it next to her bed. "Dwyn has quite a few scars, but I got to him in time. In fact, he's out and about I'm sure causing some type of mischief." He reached over and took her hand. "Trodaire is no worse for wear other than his ego. He's been worried about you all week and has been in the practice area trying to better his skill."

Raven adjusted herself again to alleviate some pain on her left side. "What about the monk?" she inquired.

Another voice came from the entrance of the tent. It was deep and gentle and seemed to be full of wisdom. "Thanks to your group, I am alive and well, young maiden."

When she looked over she saw a man dressed in a white gi that had grey sleeves and was well formed to his body, tied with a black belt. His dark skin was exotic, but seemed to sport the reminiscence of a bruise across the right side of his face. His dark hair was long and in a large pony tail that almost reached his hindquarters. His dark eyes were very mysterious and yet had compassion within them.

She nodded in the man's direction. "Master Ferric, I presume."

He returned the nod. "I am," he replied.

Raven looked to Ceartas for direction. "What happened?"

Master Ferric approached and Ceartas stood, giving the monk the chair. He looked at the bedridden exactor and asked, "May I?"

She nodded and he took the seat. Once he adjusted himself he closed his eyes and meditated for a moment. When he opened them, he explained. "During the raid, I made my way toward Norna's in order to keep her at bay."

"She really was a witch, wasn't she?" Raven interrupted, surprising the monk and Ceartas.

"Yes, but not how you think," Ferric replied.

Raven smiled briefly. "I gathered that, based on my own studies and what Maggie and Dwyn told me at Norna's shop."

The monk nodded. "Perceptive." He continued, "I was en-route to the west side of town when I came across the quartet that was slaughtering Brackus' family, so I engaged and took one down. Then Norna and Hynafin joined in the defense of Agot. Apparently I was too late in stopping her. One of the Wildmen said that they knew her human form and cast a destructive magical fireball to take out everyone. I assumed he was a wild shaman. After the explosion the shaman told the others to leave and to head to their rendezvous point. He was going to deal with Norna.

As much as I wanted to help her, I knew that if the Wildmen had more forces, Agot would not survive the night. That's when I gave chase. Ser Hynafin with her was the town's best chance in my absence. As long as her potion he drank gave him back his ability to fight the enemy, both had a chance while I dealt with the possible reinforcements.

"What do you mean 'human form"?" Raven asked.

Master Ferric sighed and looked down to his hands. "Norna was a dragon."

"Then… the lizard body!" Raven exclaimed.

"She is dead," Ferric said sadly.

Ceartas interjected, "Master Ferric, I am sorry for Norna, but that Wildman was no shaman. He was possessed by an ancient demon snake that had magic."

"Explains how it knew Norna from way back when," Raven added. She looked at the Monk. "How old was she?"

Ferric looked down at the ground for a moment then answered. "Six hundred and eight winters; very old."

Ceartas had to ask, “Why was there dragon here in Agot?”

“She lost her mate many winters before anyone settled here. When people did come to the area she put on a human disguise and made the shop, at first, a trading post. She was just looking for company because she was so lonely. There were only a few farms and a hamlet council of three when I arrived with Hynafin after our adventure with his father,” Master Ferric replied.

“How did you survive a week?” Raven inquired.

The monk turned to her. “I gave chase and engaged them just outside Agot. I was knocked out by the Wilders in a combined effort on their part. Every time I began to wake when in their custody they would just knock me out again. In between the two states of consciousness, I did, however hear them say something about possibly taking me to Strie-Kÿr. They made camp at the farm, to see if the shaman would return; he was their leader. When I finally did wake I had to break out of the cellar of the farm home you were at. I found your healer doing everything to keep you alive. That is also when I found Norna’s and Hynafin’s bodies. In order to save you though, we all had to get back here as quickly as we could. I have already dispatched the burial team to the farm and informed the next of kin earlier this week.”

Raven looked at Ceartas, “So this attack was really against the Order of the Sacred Fist, then,” she stated.

“Looks like it,” the healer replied.

Raven had a sharp pain shoot through her and she jumped a bit. The nurse healer asked all to leave to let the patient get her rest. Ceartas smiled as he left, not before opening the flap for Master Ferric to leave.

In the next few days Raven was allowed to leave the healing tent, and she slowly began her therapy to heal the damage done to her. During that time she could see Purist Amháin was unhappy with the healers letting her have leather armor instead of the platemail in order to allow proper healing of her wounds. She was just glad to be out from under its weight. She made sure she was in attendance at the training area, stretching and slowly doing her weapons exercises.

Trodaire was happy to see her and even assisted with her therapy. When he did, she gave him some pointers on how he could combat someone twice his size. He was grateful but still made a suggestive comment or two. “Is this how one can find favor with a Vadőr?" At that, she would just smile and seductively say, "One never knows…"

One time Purist Amháin heard the banter and chastised her again for such impure thoughts. He then, in order to embarrass her, made mention that because of her impurity, her wounds from her encounter was the Maker's way of showing her that she would never bear child.

It was on the evening of that insult, as the sun was going down, she was again away from the camp, by the road she was guarding when it all began. She looked toward the mountains in the distance, to home. Sitting on the soft grass next to her were Dwyn and Trodaire, both smoking Spriggan leaf.

"So…we saved the Order of the Sacred Fist?" Dwyn asked.

There was thunder to the south. Trodaire took a puff on his pipe and spoke. "Guess we did, according to Ceartas." He quickly looked south and back to the others. "I think a storm is coming."

Raven finishing her drag on the pipe, blew out the smoke then reached into her pouch and produced a small bottle and stared at it for a while. "Yes, a storm is coming. I can smell it."

Dwyn noticed her, took a drag on his pipe, and exhaled as well. "Sorry Amháin was a pain again. I should have warned you he was in the area."

"That's ok, Dwyn. He doesn't bother me anymore," she said, almost wistful.

He looked at the bottle and then all around, like they were hiding a secret from a parent. Dwyn nodded toward the bottle. "What's that?" he asked.

Trodaire looked over and then added, "Is that one of your Vadőr love potions?"

Raven just smiled as she looked at the black liquid in the bottle. She watched its sheen, almost hypnotized by its hidden power that had yet to be unleashed. She smiled seductively toward Trodaire. "No, but it will do," she said playfully.

Dwyn took one last drag on his pipe. "You didn't answer. What is that?"

The Vadőr woman stood up, took another drag on her pipe, and exhaled. She then emptied her pipe and placed it and the bottle in her pouch. Once everything was secured she looked at her two companions on the ground and smiled.

"Freedom," Raven said as she began her walk back toward Agot. "It is freedom."

The two men were watching her making her way down the hill, back to town, when another crash of thunder was heard in the distance.

Experience where it all began…

THE BLOOD WIZARD CHRONICLES NOVELLA:
STORMWIND

Screams echoed throughout the hillside as Stormwind and Carmella ran to the outskirts of Agot. Carmella yelled for Militär first, and then Rosethorn, but her voice was lost in the din of all the others. People were panic-stricken, running wildly away from the massive lumbering forms that moved between buildings.

Stormwind grabbed the arm of a woman fleeing away in fright. She wheeled on him, swinging and screaming crazily. "Whoa, whoa!" he said as he blocked her attacks. "What's happening? Who's attacking Agot?"

Terror-glazed eyes barely looked at him, only flickering to what lay beyond. "The Wilds," she muttered. "They came from the Wild lands."

Stormwind let go of the woman and let her join the throngs of other terrified townsfolk making their way toward the Order of the Sacred Fist for protection.

He looked between the escaping men and women, trying to eye their attackers. The Wild lands to the south of Agot were an almost forbidden territory. Most trade companies preferred going around the long string of mountains to the southeast. They would rather add scores of days to their journey than to risk the rolling aureate plains of the Wild lands. Creatures of disturbing size and foul ilk brooded within the serene-looking landscape.

Those vile things that lurked within the Wild lands, however, lent strength to the few foolish enough to live within. Men and women held fortified towns within the plains, surviving against all odds. Over the generations it caused the peoples within to change. Like the hard and feral monsters of the land, the men and women, too, became hard and feral. They became fearsome and barbaric, their stature in most cases rising to well over seven feet in height. These hardened peoples relished in the fight, in the violence of survival, and in the victory of life. They were often known as Wild Men, or simply Wilders, and few were ever seen outside of the borders of the Wild lands. If they were, it was often as trackers or mercenaries.

The clash of metal on metal sounded nearby bringing Stormwind out of his thoughts. He looked over in the direction of the noise. The ringing of steel against steel was rhythmic to him, almost soothing. Stormwind felt himself drawn to it. He drew his ornate rapier in a smooth motion and stepped forward. To his surprise, Carmella followed fearlessly by his side, her eyes ripping across the townscape looking desperately for her son and friend.

They rounded the corner to look into the alleyway beyond. Four men were engaged in mortal combat. It was three against one. Two of the men were the Agot guard, one a monk, and the other was indeed a Wild Man.

The Wilder towered over the others, casting them in his shadow. He was at least seven feet tall and almost three feet wide at the shoulders. He wore virtually no armor, nor clothing, instead wearing only the skins and furs of the monsters of the Wilds on his body. Stormwind could make out what looked like Sabertooth Tiger skulls on the massive man's hands, and the skin of a reptile, perhaps alligator, running over the barbarian's knees and feet. His thighs, chest, and arms were bare, showing thick, hardened muscles and a myriad of scars that were bred from countless battles. His face was hidden behind the visage of a basilisk's skull, a terrible lizard that dwelt within the Wild lands. It was said that the beast could kill by its very breath, or even with a look, and this man was wearing it's skull as a trophy. A testament to his skill in combat.

The Wild Man handled the trio of men easily, swinging his cumbersome great axe with ruthless efficiency. The man overmatched the guards before they even engaged him. Within seconds the two were cut down, their life's blood pumping hot spray against the walls of the nearby structures. The Wilder fought through the crimson mire without any regard for having taken the men's lives.

The monk, however, fought on. His skill and speed were an exemplification to the teachings of the Order of the Sacred Fist. The monk dodged the axe blows easily, maneuvering quickly between the openings the Wild Man created, to strike him in a flurry of ruthless efficiency. As Stormwind ran to his aid, he could already see welts forming across the barbarian's body where the monk had struck home. Still the monk's crushing blows did not seem to faze the barbarian in the slightest; if anything, the Wild Man seemed to fight even harder.

Stormwind managed to reach the monk's side just as the giant axe whistled through the air for his head. The nimble Elf deftly avoided the blow and struck with the speed of a cobra, plunging the thin blade up between the Wilder's ribs and piercing his heart.

Hazel eyes stared through the gruesome mask, perplexed. Stormwind understood, for he had seen the look before. The barbarian knew something was wrong, yet he felt only a pinch. Stormwind twisted the blade, opening the wound, and then yanked the sword back, removing it from the giant man's chest. Instantly the Wild Man's bewildered gaze went wide in shock and he fell to his side, dead.

Stormwind turned to the monk. "Quickly . . ." he began, but was halted. Also crumpled on the ground was the monk who had been fighting so hard. The great cleave that Stormwind had narrowly avoided had not missed the monk. It had struck true, removing the warrior priest's head from his shoulders. Stormwind felt the bile rise in his throat at the sight of the dismembered head lying only a few scant feet from the body. He turned away. There he saw Carmella staring in agony at the dead monk. She had likely known the man.

The High Elf reached gently toward her and took her olive-skinned hand. "Come on Carmella," he said quietly. "There's nothing we can do. Let's find your son."

The words brought Carmella's gaze away from her fallen compatriot. She nodded to him and said not a single word. Then they were off travelling deeper into Agot, and closer to the heart of violence.

~ ~ ~

They arrived in the market place where Stormwind had first met Carmella only two weeks before. The tables and chairs were now turned over, and it looked as if many townsfolk had barricaded themselves within the tavern. Outside, the Agot Militia fought valiantly against the overwhelming size of the enemy. Everywhere Stormwind looked, the men and even women of both the Order and Agot were fighting for their lives against the monstrous Wild Men.

Like the one that Stormwind had encountered in the alley, many of the other barbarian men were covered in the hides and furs of their conquests as well as the skulls of their triumphant victories. Some of those skulls were even humanoid.

Stormwind rushed into the fray with Carmella close behind. He fought with speed and precision and with a deft agility that even the Wild Men were not prepared for. Within moments, three of the barbarians lay dead at his feet and he prepared to advance on more. Behind him he could hear Carmella screaming for her son within the tavern. No one answered her and Stormwind feared that he knew why: Militär was not there.

Stormwind lined himself up with other members of the militia. "Do any of you know Rosethorn?" he yelled to them as they held back the advance of three more Wilders. The barbarians were learning to fear the sting of his blade and were now more reluctant to recklessly advance on him like before.

"Freckled girl?" one of the guards yelled back behind the overturned table. Stormwind tried to maneuver towards the one who had called out the vague acknowledgement but the Wild Men barred his way.

"Yes," he yelled instead. "Have you seen her?"

A Wild Man roared at Stormwind and swung his axe down to cut the Elf in half. Spittle flew from the gargantuan mouth, flinging outward like small moist projectiles. Stormwind sidestepped both. He leapt into the air and drove his rapier down between the man's clavicle and neck. The blade parted the soft flesh easily and sunk low, piercing multiple organs as it passed through his body. Stormwind removed the sword in the blink of an eye and landed gracefully back on his feet, all in a single fluid motion. The Wilder gurgled as he collapsed to the ground.

The remaining militia killed the other two barbarians and shortly after, the soldier came out from behind the table. "I tried to get her to come into the tavern, but she wouldn't listen."

Carmella, hearing the conversation ran up to Stormwind's side. "Did she have anyone with her, a small child perhaps?"

The soldier nodded. "Aye that she did. 'Fraid she wouldn't listen to me. She headed that way," he finished as he pointed east.

Stormwind looked in the direction the soldier indicated, perplexed. "But that's further away from the monastery. Would she not be trying to get to protection? Wouldn't she be trying to get Militär back to you?" he asked as he looked to Carmella.

"I don't know. She is probably just scared. Stormwind, we have to hurry! Rosethorn is not a monk, she is a local. She does not know how to defend herself. And Militär..."

Stormwind nodded; he understood. Rosethorn could walk right into a Wild Man ambush and not even see it coming. She would have no way to protect Militär then. He grabbed Carmella's hand, squeezed it once reassuringly, and then headed east through the ravaged town of Agot. Buildings were scarred with the deaths of so many. Blood graffitied the walls wherever they went and bodies littered the streets.

However, it was not a total massacre; far from it. The militia could be heard holding their ground, and for every two Agot corpses they found, they found one Wild Man. The barbarians were taking casualties, too. It was only a matter of time before the Wilders would have to declare the battle a rout and withdraw. Stormwind did not think Rosethorn and Militär had that kind of time though.

They looked in every house they passed by and Carmella would call out to the two of them. Still he had not heard a response from either. Nevertheless, one thing he did notice was that they were encountering the Wilders far less frequently. It looked as if the eastern end of the town had been the first to feel the effects of the raid and now the core of the Wild Man advance had held firm in the center of town. It made it easier to search for Carmella's son, and if Militär were around, he would find him.

The two reached the edge of town. Beyond, all that Stormwind could see were farms and tilled fields. If Rosethorn and Militär were cutting through the farmland, Stormwind's keen elven sight would be able to see them but as it was, there was no one to be found. Everyone that was not fighting had fled to the monastery to the west. He turned and looked to the woman whose child he was trying to save. "Did Rosethorn know the farmers well? Would she take Militär to a barn perhaps?" he asked, and then turned to look at the tracks on the ground.

He already knew the answer before she said anything, though. Fresh tracks were only coming in; none were leaving. The tracks inward were also massive depressions that he had gathered came from the footfalls of the Wild Men. There was nothing so small that it denoted that it came from a child or a young woman. Still he waited for Carmella's answer.

"No," she remarked. "Perhaps we missed them somehow," she said with a reserve of calm Stormwind was amazed she had.

"They could have doubled back towards the monastery. Perhaps someone convinced Rosethorn to head there?"

The High Elf watched as the dark-haired beauty bit her lower lip in frustration. "Perhaps," she agreed.

Stormwind began to turn back when suddenly he saw a flicker of movement. The Elf reacted on impulse, pushing Carmella out of the way and diving to the side just as three shards of ebony stone tore through the wooden fencing that they had just been standing near.

Stormwind ended his dive in a roll and came to his feet, his ornate rapier ready. Carmella, however, was not as graceful when she hit the ground.

Stormwind's cerulean eyes scanned the cluster of houses behind him. Carmella and he had just looked in every one and they were empty. From where had the attack come? Then he saw it: the silhouette of a woman in a doorway some twenty feet away. How had he missed that? He heard a chanting sound as she raised her hands once more. Instinct forced him to spin away from her and around the corner of a nearby home. Brick and mortar exploded outward from the edge of the house as another trio of sharp obsidian shards ripped through the building, as if it had no more consistency than wet paper.

He knew what it was then: Magic. The assailer was a sorceress of some kind.

"Krake, finish him," he heard a vaguely familiar voice say from around the corner.

Stormwind pushed himself up against the wall and slowly crouched. His gut told him that he should flank around the building and try to attack the assailers from behind, but as he glanced to Carmella lying prone on the ground he knew he could not leave her behind.

Then a large bone-plated leg stepped into his view of the fallen monk. Stormwind followed it upward to the largest human he had ever seen in his life.

The man had to be close to seven and a half feet tall, his shoulder span reaching almost four feet across. Thick heavy muscle rippled across the huge Wild Man's body through pockets of leather and fur that were patchworked amidst his towering frame. The skulls of basilisks resided on each shoulder, and his dark grey orbs stared down at Stormwind through the skull of an armor-plated crown of a gorgon. Two long horns rose off on both sides of the skull and jutted forward like hooked javelins. Stormwind could see a tangled black beard sticking out from beneath the gorgon mask.

"You must be Krake," he said dryly as the Wild Man roared at him and swung a colossal poleaxe with both hands. The agile Elf easily rolled away from the hulking monstrosity of a man before him and came to his feet once more almost six feet away.

Krake spun around instantly, rolling the poleaxe around easily with the skill of a master. Stormwind looked at the long weapon with a well of fear growing in the pit of his stomach. The poleaxe was over six feet in length with an axe head, a haft of a hammer, and spike tip across the top. It was a versatile weapon and one that hindered the Elf. The barbarian had range and size on Stormwind, and the Elf needed to be close to be effective.

Krake swung the poleaxe in a wide arc, Stormwind barely managing to duck out of the way of the curved blade, when the immense warrior instantly followed through with a crushing slam of his hammer. Stormwind narrowly escaped the pulverizing attack as the hammer head slammed into the cobblestone road, shattering the smooth stones into fragmented slivers and dust.

Stormwind attempted to gain his footing but the Wild Man vigorously advanced. The Elf backpedaled frantically as axe fall followed a swing of a hammer, followed by the stab of the spear tip. It was as if there was no escaping the overpowering goliath. Finally, the deft Elf managed to flip over a small fence to grant him a modicum of room before the Wilder shattered it, too, with a swing of the hammer. Stormwind could not believe the man's speed and endurance for his size. It seemed inhuman!

The Wilder pushed forward, confidence gleaming in his dark glare as he forced Stormwind into retreat again and again. Stormwind thought for sure that the Wild Man was invincible, when he made his first mistake. As he stabbed forward, he kept the hammerhead facing his opponent and the axe away. Stormwind realized the strategy, for if the Elf dodged to the outside, as the Wilder expected, he could follow through with a sweep attack from the axe, effectively hamstringing the Elf. Stormwind was not going to give him the luxury. When the piece came forward again, instead of dodging to the side, he moved forward.

He spun wide letting the sharp spike slide along the inside of his armor. As he came around he caught the hammer haft and used it as leverage to hurtle himself forward. Within the Wild Man's perimeter and against the weapon, the massive man was defenseless. With all his strength, he stabbed forward. His thin blade perforated the seams of the Wilder's muscled flesh and drove completely through his body, erupting in a crimson explosion as the tip exited his back.

To Stormwind's surprise, the Wild Man did not so much as grunt. Instead, with amazing willpower, Krake dropped his poleaxe and instead grabbed Stormwind, who was so close to the goliath he could not escape in time.

Krake's hands locked onto Stormwind's shoulders, binding his arms in place. With unbelievable strength, he lifted Stormwind from the ground. The grip on his arms was excruciating. Stormwind tried to hold onto his rapier but found the lock on his arms too tight and felt his grip ripped away.

Stormwind knew that things had taken a turn for the worse, but still he did not relent. As the hulking monstrosity squeezed down on him, crushing the air from his lungs, the Elf kicked as hard as he could against the man's flank. If the Wild Man noticed at all, it did not even register. Krake lifted Stormwind up so that the Elf was looking through the eyeholes of the gorgon skull to the man underneath. It was a visage of death. He knew this was the end, yet he remained defiant. With all the power he could muster, he spit into the eyehole.

Krake drove the skull helmet down on Stormwind's head. Searing pain and bright light exploded all around and everything began spinning. He felt the crushing blow again and the light was now replaced with stars. Then he was falling.

The ground rushed up to greet him and he slammed down hard on his side with a cry of pain. The world spun and swerved before him and lights danced all around. He felt hot fluid pouring liberally across his head and down his face. He looked up at the monster above him.

Pain ran through his body like lightning, coursing from his neck down to his toes. Still he watched as the Wild Man slowly reached down to his own abdomen and removed Stormwind's rapier. He made no sound and Stormwind could only watch as the cruor-covered blade slid wetly from the barbarian's body. When the tip finally emerged, a red gout of blood followed it. It was then that Krake grunted. He put his hand over the crimson-drenched wound and threw Stormwind's rapier down.

The Elf tried to move, but his body would not respond. He could only watch as Krake picked up the poleaxe once more. He arced the axe head towards Stormwind's neck, and with one hand raised the weapon for a felling blow. The blade began to race downward.

"Wait!" a woman's voice called.

The blade stopped only inches from Stormwind's face. He stared at the glinting metal hovering so closely above him.

Suddenly a freckled female's hand came into view as she pushed the weapon away from his face. She bent over and smiled wickedly down at him, her green eyes glittering in triumph. "Well... well... well... what an unexpected surprise? And to think I thought it was actually the Agot Militia giving my Wilders such a hard time. I should have figured it to be a High Elf."

He watched helplessly as another Wild Man walked by with an unconscious Militär hanging limply from his shoulder. His gaze fell back to the woman as tears began to stream out of his eyes in shock. She stood up, "Goodbye, Stormwind."

~ ~ ~

Continue the saga in the novella- Stormwind, A Blood Wizard Chronicles Novella, available at Amazon.com, CreateSpace.com, on Amazon Kindle, and at www.AuthorJayErickson.com

If you enjoyed this novel, please take a moment and review it favorably. Every bit helps.

Thank you.

Jay Erickson
J. P. Strohm
Authors

~~~
~~~

ABOUT THE AUTHORS

JAY ERICKSON grew up in Midwestern USA before joining the United States Air Force at the age of nineteen as an aircraft mechanic. In 2001, he separated from active service and became an Air Force Reservist.

Since that time, he has held a variety of jobs from working at a casino, to operating cranes, to laying brick. Even with a myriad of different careers, though, writing has been his primary interest and hobby. As an avid reader, he has always held a deep love for Fantasy and Science Fiction. It was a natural fit for his writing. Now he's taking that hobby one step further by joining Halsbren Publishing LLC and releasing his saga THE BLOOD WIZARD CHRONICLES for others to read. Mr. Erickson resides in Northwest Indiana with his wife and two children.

~ ~ ~

J.P. STROHM has always had a love for fantasy stories and science fiction, one of the first books he ever read was J.R.R. Tolkien's "The Hobbit". He is an avid gamer of Dungeons and Dragons since the 1980's, and an owner of the original Red Box Basic Set. It was through that gaming that he learned how to weave stories that captivated the hearts of his gaming groups.

In 2015, JAY ERICKSON requested to introduce his style of writing into the newly created world of KULDARR. J.P. STROHM graciously accepted.

J.P. STROHM has served in the United States military for over twenty years, and was born in the state of Indiana. Mr. Strohm is married to his wife, Susan, and has two children; Katherine and Crystal.

www.ingramcontent.com/pod-product-compliance
Lightning Source LLC
Chambersburg PA
CBHW030334310726
48979CB00001B/30

* 9 7 8 1 9 4 2 9 5 8 0 6 2 *